KNIFE EDGE

Brad Winters, ramrod of the Block F ranch, only wants to do his job. However, his boss Matt Farrell has other ideas: he wants to re-enact the Battle of Hashknife Ridge, which had been fought there fifteen years earlier. It means a meeting of North and South — and old hatreds are far from buried. Before the battle begins there are shootings, robberies and assassination attempts. And by the time it's over, the wonder is that there is anybody left alive.

Books by Tyler Hatch
in the Linford Western Library:

A LAND TO DIE FOR
BUCKSKIN GIRL
DEATHWATCH TRAIL
LONG SHOT
VIGILANTE MARSHAL
FIVE GRAVES WEST
BIG BAD RIVER
CHETENNE GALLOWS
DEAD WHERE YOU STAND!
DURANGO GUNHAWK

TYLER HATCH

KNIFE EDGE

Complete and Unabridged

LINFORD
Leicester

First published in Great Britain in 2007 by
Robert Hale Limited
London

First Linford Edition
published 2008
by arrangement with
Robert Hale Limited
London

British Library CIP Data

Hatch, Tyler
  Knife edge.—Large print ed.—
  Linford western library
  1. Western stories
  2. Large type books
  I. Title
  823.9′2 [F]

ISBN 978–1–84782–431–8

Published by
F. A. Thorpe (Publishing)
Anstey, Leicestershire

Set by Words & Graphics Ltd.
Anstey, Leicestershire
Printed and bound in Great Britain by
T. J. International Ltd., Padstow, Cornwall

This book is printed on acid-free paper

1

First Blood

'What the hell . . . ?'

The words exploded from the rider topping-out on the hogback rise above the meandering and cool timber-lined river that lay in the shadow of Hashknife Ridge. The rough-looking cowboy hauled rein now and hipped in the saddle. Thin lips mostly hidden by a drooping, tobacco-stained moustache, he turned his head and called down to the rider coming up the slope behind.

'Brad! Come look at this!' He pointed, as the rider below, responding to the alarm and urgency in the man's voice, touched spurs to the flanks of his buckskin gelding.

'What we got, Kit?'

Kit tugged at his moustache while he waited for Brad to come up alongside,

1

then pointed down through the timber. 'Somethin' white down there — looks like — damned if it don't look like tents!'

Brad Winters, saddle-tall, slab-shouldered, tilted his stained curl-brim hat forward over his eyes, cutting the glare. He was a man in his mid-thirties, weathered, square-jawed. Grey eyes narrowed now as his wide mouth moved in a silent oath. 'Dammit! They're early!'

Kit Turner stiffened. 'Aw, not them blue-bellies already!'

Winters was already over the rise and putting the gelding down the slope, working back and forth in short zigzags: no cowman worth his salt sent a working horse careering down a gravel slope, not even one as short as this. But Kit Turner had no such scruples, set his shaggy roan straight down, the animal's rear legs folding so the haunches almost scraped the ground, sliding. Dust boiled up behind.

As he passed Winters, the younger man said, 'Why not fire a couple of shots, just to make sure they know we're coming, Kit!'

Turner flushed, hauled rein — but it was too late. Through the vegetation they could see men running about down there at the cluster of small tents pitched along the river bank. They were facing this way and three at least held rifles, blued metal glinting in the sunlight of early autumn.

Coming out of the treeline, Brad Winters held up a gloved hand. 'Easy now.' His grey eyes ran along the line of men, a few in ordinary range clothes, most wearing various parts of uniforms of the Union Army. He picked the leader, a tall, bulky man, standing spraddle-legged in his tight, striped trousers and half-boots, dark-blue suspenders over his unbuttoned undershirt. No rank insignia — and no welcome on that rugged face.

'Who're you?' His voice was booming, coming out of the deep chest, a handful of hair showing at the undershirt neck opening.

Winters ignored the question. 'You're

not s'posed to be here till next week.'

'So we're early. Colonel said to get the lay of the land, set up camp.' The man grinned coldly. 'Bein' only a lowly lieutenant, I do what I'm told.'

Winters nodded. 'Good — so haul down your tents and move out and come back next week.'

The Union men stirred restlessly, but looked to the lieutenant for guidance. The big man twisted heavy lips into a crooked smile. 'Helluva lot of trouble to go to. We've kinda lost the knack of pitchin' tents, not bein' in the real army no more. These took us a long time to put up.'

'Call this a practice session then. You'll be able to set 'em up quicker and better next week.'

The lieutenant pursed his lips as if giving the matter some thought. 'Nah — we got 'em about right now. Reckon we'll just leave 'em be.'

'You won't.'

The lieutenant's pale-blue eyes narrowed. 'Mister, this is my camp. I'll decide what we do or don't do.'

Winters shook his head and Turner licked his lips: he knew that stubborn look on the other's face. 'Not this time. We're driving in a bunch of cattle to graze here for a week or so. Your tents are in the way, right on the lushest grass.'

'Plenty grass along there, closer to the ridge.'

'Sure, but see how short it is? Been grazed already. This is where we need to hold our cows.'

The big man sighed. 'Look, friend, it don't make sense to me. It's gonna be a battleground in a week . . . ' The lieutenant suddenly squinted. 'Ah! I get it! Still playin' Johnny Reb, huh? Roust the poor ol' Yankee!'

Winters shook his head. 'I never heard of any 'poor' ol' Yankees. War's been over fifteen years, for Chris'sake.'

'But you rednecks still can't stomach that we furled your rebel flag for you, can you?' The Union men chuckled, one man guffawing loudly. It pleased the lieutenant.

'Not at Hashknife Ridge, you didn't,' Winters said.

The big Yankee's grin widened. 'Aw, we'll whup your asses next week. Easy!'

His men cheered this time.

Winters smiled crookedly. 'It's s'posed to be a *re-enactment* of an historical event — you Yankees lost here at Hashknife in '64, even though you outnumbered us nigh three to one. *And* had better weapons and supplies. But you couldn't take the Ridge.' He gestured vaguely with his left hand to the high slopes of Hashknife. 'Couldn't get past the reb line. And you won't this time, either, even though it's only staged. We'll make sure history repeats itself.'

Kit Turner figured it was time he put in his two cents' worth. 'Ran with your tails between your legs in '64 — guess you'd had plenty of practice. Sure looked like it, anyways.'

Winters motioned to Kit to ease off without looking at the cowboy: he watched the tension building in the

6

men facing him, focused again on the stiff-faced lieutenant.

'I'm Brad Winters.'

The man frowned. 'That ain't the name of the feller I was told owns this land.'

'No, that's Matt Farrell. He owns Block F — I'm his ramrod.'

'Then what'm I doin' talkin' to you? I don't deal with the help. Where's this Farrell?'

'Busy. You got a name?'

'Joe Briscoe — Sometimes called *Big Joe*.'

'Wonder why?' someone in the ranks called and got a rippling chuckle. Briscoe seemed to like it, too.

'Well, Joe, you let your enthusiasm get the better of you. You're way too early and you'll have to move.'

Briscoe folded his arms, bulging his muscles through the undershirt. 'The colonel will decide that. He'll be along in the next coupla days.'

Winters nodded slowly, his gaze fixed on the big man's face now. 'You can hardly wait, can you?' he said softly. 'You want to get at our throats again: only you aim to change history this time, right? At the Battle of Hashknife Ridge, in 1864, a small troop of Confederates turned back over a hundred of you Yankees. They were ready to fight to the last man, but you blue-bellies decided to call it quits instead. That's how it happened and that's how it'll stay in the books and records. No point in restaging it otherwise.'

Briscoe's face was heavy with suffusing blood now. 'The retreat was orders! None of the colonel's doin'! We'd've wiped you out if only they'd let us stay.'

'Coupla big words, them, ain't they? *If only*. Two of the most used words in the language, I'd say.' Winters sighed. 'Well, it didn't happen that way and, far as I'm concerned, it hardly matters now.'

'Matters to you damn Rebs! Or you wouldn't've set up this re-enactment!'

'Well, it wasn't to make you Yanks

look better. Town businessmen see it as a way to bring in a lot of free-spending visitors, make everyone rich. Most folk seem to think it's a good idea.'

'You?'

Winters shrugged. 'Makes no never-mind to me. I wasn't in the original battle. You want the truth, I figure this is all one big damn nuisance. I got a ranch to run, cows to round-up and fatten for market. Having to work around a bunch of fellers playing at soldiers in a battle that was fought fifteen years ago, don't fill me with much joy. So, let's not have any trouble, Briscoe. Haul down your tents and come back in a week's time, save everyone a lot of trouble.'

Briscoe was silent for a few moments, hands on hips, jaw thrusting. 'Tell you what, Winters — you go to hell!'

'Guess I'm headed that way, but not right now!'

The spurs chinked briefly as they drove into the startled gelding. It leaped forward with a whinny and Big Joe

Briscoe hurled himself sideways, but not quite fast enough. The buckskin hit him and he was sent flying several feet, rolling and cussing. Some of the rifles came up but Winters ignored them as he quit the saddle and charged in at Briscoe, a man who would want to do his own fighting. He was struggling to his feet, about halfway up, when Brad slammed the first blow to the side of the big, heavy jaw. The man's head snapped sideways and Winters stepped in, hammered two more punches to Briscoe's face. His arms blurred as he pistoned a barrage into the Yankee's ribcage and midriff.

Big Joe was gasping and gagging as he dropped to his knees.

'Steady there, you blue-bellies!' roared Kit Turner, showing the men with rifles the sawn-off shotgun he had taken from a leather saddle boot. 'Just empty your hands, step on back and watch.'

They obeyed, faces tight and pale, but mighty leery of that shotgun. Most seemed stunned that Briscoe was on the receiving end of those hard fists.

Big Joe was on his feet now, bleeding, shaking his head, fists like lumps of knotted granite. He spat some blood to one side and actually grinned as he strode forward to meet Winters' next charge. He parried the first blow, raising his left forearm fast, hooking a punch to the ramrod's chest. Winters felt as if he had been kicked by his horse and staggered back, breath going out of him with a *whoosh!* He almost went down, fought to keep balance. Yankee yells encouraged Big Joe and he stepped in confidently, fists cocked.

Winters got purchase with one boot and launched himself at the big lieutenant. It caught Briscoe off-guard but he turned a large hip into Winters, stopping him in his tracks, then hammered two merciless blows at the ramrod's head, knocking off his hat. Kit Turner's moan of despair was quite audible above all the yelling.

But, though shaken by the big man's defence, Winters didn't go down

— except voluntarily to one knee. And as Briscoe was carried forward by his own momentum, Winters came up as if shot from a mortar, his fist cracking under Big Joe's jaw. The man's head snapped back like it would break his neck. His feet did a brief, unco-ordinated dance and he started to fall. Winters turned side on, whipping his left hand from behind his back, spinning his body at the same time towards the Yankee. His arm hurt clear to the shoulder as his knuckles thudded into the muscles of Briscoe's thick neck.

Joe went down heavily, rolling a little, but toppled back towards the ramrod. Winters drove a boot into the big chest, spinning him hard. Groggily, only stubborn spirit driving him to fight on, Big Joe stumbled up, fists hammering, rocking Winters. The ramrod ducked and weaved, only allowed Briscoe to stand partly upright as he delivered his punches. They lost some of their sting this way because the big man was unable to throw his full weight behind them. Maybe that was why he scooped up gravel and flung it into Winters' face. The ramrod jumped back, but suddenly lunged forward again, kicked Joe in the hip. As the big Yankee began to sprawl, Brad clipped him on the side of the jaw with a sledging, downward blow. Briscoe, his fall given savage impetus by the cowman's whistling punch, hit the ground so hard his face drove into the dirt and sent gravel spraying.

Brad Winters was unsteady on his feet, the left side of his face swollen, already darkening. He looked — and felt — like a man who had been on the wrong end of a pick-axe handle. He worked his jaw painfully and shook his left hand with its bleeding, split knuckles. But Briscoe was unmoving, except for heavy, ragged breathing making his huge ribcage bulge and deflate.

One of the Yankees suddenly dived for his rifle as Kit looked down at

Briscoe, admiring Winters' handiwork. The cowboy, Kit, didn't see the move, but Winters caught a blur out of the corner of his eye and spun, right hand instinctively reaching for his six-gun. It cleared leather at the same time as the Yankee got his Winchester across his chest, levering. The man panicked and pulled the trigger while the barrel was slanted skywards — and that was where his bullet went. Winters' lead burned across the man's upper arm, throwing him onto his back.

'Next man tries anything gets it dead-square,' Winters said: his bullet hitting the Yankee at all was a plain fluke, but he saw no reason to admit that. The men lifted their hands, the wounded one staggering upright, holding his bleeding arm. Winters jerked the Colt's smoking barrel.

'Dismantle the tents and pack up. Then move out: I'll give you twenty minutes.'

'What the hell you think we are?' one man growled. 'We been outa the army for years! This is just a — a bit of fun we volunteered for — or we figured it would be!'

'Fun starts next week,' Winters told them coolly. 'Your time starts *now!*'

As the grumbling men swore and blundered their way through the chores, Big Joe Briscoe came out of it slowly. He was uglier than ever now, his nose slanted towards the right side of his face, eyes puffy, thick lips split and some skin torn off his cheek by the gravel. His eyes were a little glazed as he looked around, watching his men pack away the tents. Then he saw Winters and his gaze sharpened. He lifted a hand and shook a big sausage of a finger at the ramrod.

'I'm lookin' forward to next week, Winters! You got any sense, you'll load live ammo instead of blanks!'

'No need. If I can't kick your Yankee butt clear over Hashknife, I'll sign on as your camp cook.'

Big Joe grinned crookedly, showing blood-smeared teeth. 'I'm sure lookin' forward to the new Battle of Hashknife Ridge, feller, but I doubt that Colonel Endicott would trust a lousy Reb to prepare his meals!'

Briscoe's words cut off sharply and he frowned. Kit Turner showed some surprise, too, at the expression that suddenly tightened Winters' battered features into hard, white, angular planes.

'Endicott? That couldn't be *Kel* Endicott?'

Briscoe held his frown a mite longer then grinned widely. 'Ain't you in for a surprise!'

'Can't be the man I'm thinking of! That Endicott died on a munitions train that blew up!'

'Judas, Brad!' breathed Turner, feeling his skin prickle as he watched the change that had come over the ramrod. 'What the hell's the matter?'

'Think you've met our colonel before, eh, Winters?' Briscoe asked, interested now, but with a kind of smirk.

Brad shook his head briefly. 'I guess not.'

Big Joe frowned briefly. 'Well, that's another pleasure you've yet to enjoy!' He laughed aloud and spat again. 'He just *loves* Johnny Rebs!'

'Not this one, he won't,' Winters said, and jerked the six-gun again. 'Come on — those tents're tied on good enough. Climb into leather and light a shuck, pronto.'

'They sure got a queer way of talkin' down here, eh, boys?' Briscoe said, swinging stiffly into saddle, having two tries before he was successful. But, though it was obviously painful, it didn't seem to faze the big man any as he tugged on the reins. 'Brad Winters, huh?'

'Name won't mean anything to Endicott.' Winters' voice was raspy and Turner saw his left hand was clenched so tight the knuckles were white.

'I wonder . . . Well, see you in the battle, I hope, Reb. I dunno about the rest, but you and me'll be goin' at it like it was the original Hashknife fight! OK with you?'

Winters didn't answer, nostrils white and pinched. He watched with narrowed eyes as the Yankees forded the river and rode slowly away down the valley.

Turner wiped his damp face with a neckerchief, holstering the scattergun. 'Whew! Never knew you hated Yankees so much, Brad.'

'Only some,' Winters replied, not taking his eyes off the slowly disappearing Union men.

Turner started to speak, changed his mind, but thought, *Yeah — an' one of 'em's this Colonel Kel Endicott, whoever he is. I wonder what the hell he ever did to old Brad . . . ?*

2

Old Blood

Matt Farrell was dressed in his town clothes, white shirt with string tie, striped trousers tucked into the tops of dust-coated halfboots. His good buff-coloured curl-brim hat dangled on the stand beside the desk in the cramped ranch office and he dodged it expertly as he sat down in the big leather-padded chair. He looked younger than Brad Winters — he was, but only by about three months — and his smooth skin and freshly barbered dark hair helped his appearance. His face was almost perfectly oval, a thin nose separating steady brown eyes, jaw jutting just a little now as he looked at his foreman.

'Brad, don't you foul this show up for me, or I'll forget you were my lieutenant in the War and kick your butt outa here.'

Winters smiled crookedly, pulling out a straight-back chair and dropping into it. 'Now, Sergeant, that's no way to speak to your superior officer.'

Farrell smiled, but not all that warmly.

'Well, we've been friends for a lot of years, Brad, and I don't want to have a falling-out with you over this Hashknife Ridge thing.' He paused to light a cheroot, pushing the box across to Winters who helped himself and lit up from a match scraped across his boot. 'I know you're against this re-enactment but it's going to be good for the town, mighty good. And that means the ranch'll benefit, too.'

'Oh, I can see it'll bring in a lot of money, Matt. Far as I know there's never been anything like it before, leastways not staged full-scale. The medicine shows have a tableau occasionally of a part of some famous battle, but this is gonna spread halfway across our range — *that's* what I'm agin. It's gonna throw our work out all to hell.'

'We can manage, and it'll only be the one day, October ten.'

'One day staging the actual battle, but for a week or more we're gonna have dozens of Yankees and local volunteers wanting to dress up as Rebs camped on our range — all eager to fight, even it is only with blanks and wooden bayonets — hell, you even brought in a couple of cannon.'

Farrell's smile widened and he sat back, looking mighty pleased with himself. 'Both were used in the original battle in '64, right out on the Ridge there. Adds a lot to the show. You'd be surprised at how many folk remember this fight, Brad — I mean, it is something to be proud of. Less than forty Rebs beat off over a hundred Yankees and were actually on their last boxes of bullets when the blue-bellies retreated. I mean, that must've been real dyed-in-the-wool humiliation when the Union Army learned that! If they'd hung on just a coupla hours longer . . . '

'Yankee pride's got a long memory, Matt, they could see this as another chance to square it away.'

'No, no,' Farrell said confidently. 'This'll be just for entertainment. War's over, remember?' He spread his arms and laughed, sitting up straight now, looking right at his foreman. 'You know, I can still feel a touch of steel in my spine when I think about that fight, or hear good ol' songs of the South, Brad. Hell, I'm mighty proud to be a Southerner. I *like* to be called 'Reb'. I'm proud of my heritage, and you should be, too.'

Winters nodded, dusting ash from his cheroot into the buffalo horn tray on the desk. 'I know all that, Matt, and I know your businessmen friends in town feel the same way. I got no beef about the town making money, it's just that the whole damn show is gonna be on our land and it's gonna wreck our schedule. We're gonna have to clean up after it all, too, for Chris'sake, lose more time.'

'Aah, you work too hard, Brad! I'm always telling you to take some time off, go into town, kick over the traces a little. *Relax*, man! Get some enjoyment out of life. There's more to it than sweat and saddle-sores.'

Winters said nothing. Matt Farrell had come from a well-to-do family in Georgia, and had been a good sergeant during the war: actually surprising Winters how comfortably he took orders from him, a rough-neck drifter, who'd been lucky enough to wipe out a Yankee gun position in a few moments of madness and earn himself a promotion in-the-field. Yes, they'd been friends for a long time and when Farrell had written him and said he'd bought the Block F and wanted him for his foreman — well, it had come just at the right time when he'd had his butt showing through his trousers and old newspapers stuffed in his boots to cover the holes worn in the soles.

It was strange at first — the sergeant now giving the lieutenant orders — but the comradeship from the army saw them through smoothly. Matt was a rich man and Block F had expanded, eventually taking in Hashknife Ridge, the old revered battlefield where the Confederates had had a truly resounding victory over the hated Union forces.

Now, on the fifteenth anniversary of that day of blood and battle, it was about to be staged again, with the backing of Block F and the Town Council, which comprised most of the local businessmen, and the Cattlemen's Alliance. A lot of money was available for a good show — and to pay for plenty of publicity. *And, it was hoped, a lot more money would pour into the county.*

The word had spread rapidly and everyone concerned was well and truly surprised at the interest shown. Folk were promising to come from all over, not just this south-eastern corner of Colorado, but from Texas, Georgia, Tennessee, Kentucky, Mississippi, Missouri, South Carolina — the whole South had been stirred: anything to take another poke at the despised, all-conquering Yankees: *the South had a long memory*.

In town, new rooming-houses had been built, one three storeys high, which was an added attraction: a building that size in a frontier town was something to gawk at. Another saloon was nearing completion: the whore-house had been redecorated — now that would be something to see! Hash-houses and cafés were opening all over. Folk cleared out junk rooms, even tool sheds, and fitted them out for human habitation — at a price, a *higher* price. The livery built larger holding pens. The bank ordered a huge newfangled combination vault in antici-pation of providing adequate safe holding facilities for all the extra cash that was expected to be deposited, even if only temporarily. The sheriff had three permanent deputies, with four more temporaries on stand-by.

Yes, it was going to be the biggest day this neck of the woods had ever seen since — well, since the original Battle of Hashknife Ridge, 10 October 1864.

Most folk figured Remembrance Day, as it was officially called, was going to make everyone rich.

'You have to savvy you can't stop this, Brad,' Farrell said suddenly, breaking into Winters' drifting thoughts.

'I know, Matt, I'm not really trying to do that: hell, they'd lynch me from the new whorehouse gate if I did! I guess I figured those Yankees were setting up camp just to show us they weren't doing us any favours by joining in the deal, that they were calling the shots — that didn't set easy with my Southern blood.'

'Well, I guess we expected there was always gonna be some friction between locals and true Yankees who'd actually fought at the Ridge coming back for the show.' He waved a finger at his ramrod. 'But, Brad, you've drawn first blood and it's still a week to go. Council's not happy about that.'

Winters sighed, stubbed out his

cheroot. 'Yeah, well, I only wanted to get our herd moved in and grazing — never thought about the hassle it'd cause.'

Farrell nodded, then waved a hand. 'Hell, we can smooth it over if we need to.' He paused, flicked his brown gaze to Winters' face. 'Kit said there was something about you and this Yankee colonel who's coming in to take charge . . . Got you riled-up?'

Winters composed his face and kept it carefully blank. 'Not riled, just puzzled. Man named Endicott. Heard of him during the war, before you joined the outfit and, far as I knew he'd been blown to bits in a munitions' train explosion — I was surprised to hear he was still alive, that's all.'

'That bother you?' Farrell asked shrewdly, but Winters shook his head slowly.

'No.' There was little that could be read into that single, clipped denial.

Farrell tapped fingers against his desk edge, eyes steady. 'I don't recall our outfit ever going up against a Yankee by that name.'

'We never did, far as I know.' Winters heaved to his feet. 'I just heard he was on the train that blew up on the high trestle at Deacon's Drop, the one the Yankees had disguised as a hospital train but filled it with ammo. I wouldn't think anyone could've survived. Now I better get Rankin and Dumplin' Dan moving that herd into the Hashknife before dark.'

Farrell's face was sober: it was plain he wasn't really satisfied with his ramrod's answer, but he knew he wouldn't improve on it by further questioning. 'OK — but if you find any more Yankees setting-up camp, don't lynch 'em, OK?' He grinned. 'Ask 'em politely if they'd be so good as to leave and come back in a week's time when we'll bend over backwards to make 'em feel at home.'

Winters threw a mocking salute as he went out, saying, 'I'll be sure to do that, boss.'

Farrell continued to stare at the closed door, still frowning, lightly tapping his fingers on his desk.

'Brad,' he said softly, 'you're a bad liar, pard. Mostly, I suspect, because it just ain't your style.'

★ ★ ★

He hadn't had the dream for years, but it came to him again that night. In every blazing detail.

The place was called Pincushion, because of the swarms of cactus studding the landscape. They were in the wild Chavez country of New Mexico, the western edge of the Llano Estacado within sight . . .

It had been a quiet patrol so far for Brad Winters and his scouts. Then the big Irish sergeant, O'Malley, had spotted a glow in amongst the low hills. Wary investigation had brought them up with a camp of Southern boys in charge of a Major Hartmann.

'We can feed you tonight, Winters,

29

but we're husbanding our supplies. Still have a lot of patrol to complete yet. Searching for a missing scout.' Hartmann was a top-heavy man and seemed to like to keep himself moving constantly on his skinny legs. He twirled his bushy moustache and Winters thought he detected some sort of accent there: maybe Limey. 'But we'd be glad of your company for a few days if you can spare the time . . . Indians watching from the ridges, you know.' He lowered his voice, adding, 'And I have it on good authority that the Yankees are somewhere in the vicinity.'

'That's what I've been ordered to check out,' Brad told the man, but there was no more discussion about military matters until supper was over.

Then, while his men exchanged gossip with Hartmann's troopers, Winters sat on a tree trunk, smoking with the major. He was able to give the man news of Yankee movements to the north and east.

'We think they're going to try and

take over the trestle bridge at Deacon's Drop. Appears they're establishing a station up on the Llano so they can control the pass. Fixing a supply line is gonna be hard for 'em, though. They're a long way from any back-up.'

'Just so.' Hartmann drew on his pipe: it had a large bowl with a silver rim. 'We're stationed at Fort Balcombe but our position is very tentative. Indians gathering and, we suspect, being supplied with arms by the Union forces. An attack on the fort seems imminent. We sent out a scout, young feller, but experienced. Seem to've lost him, so locating him is part of my job. The rest is to gather information about the whereabouts of the Union forces in this area.'

The word ended abruptly, not fully-formed, because there was a single shot and a bullet exploded the big pipe bowl and continued on to plough into Hartmann's chest. The sound of the shot was followed quickly by the blood-curdling war cries of attacking

Indians, who seemed to be urged on by white men. Winters dropped behind the log, fumbling his Gunnison and Griswald revolver out of his holster. A glance told him that Hartmannn was dead. No, they weren't just Indians — horsemen in Yankee uniforms rode with them. But the Indians had their own agenda and came leaping and racing in afoot, swinging hatchets and clubs as well as firing the cumbersome muskets the Yankees had given them. Obviously they hadn't taken time to properly train the redskins in the use of the firearms, and this was probably what saved the Confederates: Indian savagery simply wasn't enough to ensure a victory.

Winters rolled onto his side, shot a man leaping over the log, the limbs thrashing wildly as he fell. Another dark shape launched itself, only a couple of feet beyond where Winters lay. He thrust out the smoking pistol, felt the barrel jar on something and dropped the hammer. The gun bucked hard against his wrist and he knew the muzzle was buried in flesh when it fired. He managed to hold onto the weapon, kicked the dead Indian off him and rolled away, coming up to one knee. Shadows writhed and leapt and screamed all around him, shapes blurring against the stars. The camp-fire had been kicked apart and the scattered glowing coals resembled stars fallen to earth. The pistol was empty and he flung it into a snarling copper face, snatched the man's rifle as he fell.

It was a heavy, long-barrelled musket and Winters gripped it by the hot muzzle end and swung as a mounted soldier rode in, shooting down at him. The bullet seared his forehead, knocking him off balance, brilliant lights bursting behind his eyes. He kept the rifle swing going instinctively, felt it jerk solidly, the gun almost torn from his grip. There was a grunt and the soldier toppled onto him. He kicked free, staggering up, felt another bullet whip air past his face. He jumped back so fast he stumbled and fell.

Men were fighting hand-to-hand all around him, some still mounted — Yankees, he guessed — and riding in, striking with swords or gun butts. He cast around him wildly, looking for a weapon, preferably loaded, knowing the attackers were winning. 'Find the kid, damn you!' a Yankee voice bellowed.

Then there was a crashing volley of rifle fire and horses shrilled as they were knocked off their feet, went down thrashing and rolling, throwing their riders. A second volley crashed and someone made a whimpering sound. Seconds later a Yankee voice bawled urgently, 'Fall back! Fall back!'

There was chaos, horses and men running around wildly, cannoning into each other, blinded by the heavy pall of powdersmoke, stumbling over dead bodies. Winters found a Colt pistol on the body of a Yankee sergeant and he fired all three remaining shots after the retreating men but wasn't sure he hit anyone.

Panting, sweating, he joined the others, taking time to say, 'Fine defence, men. They caught us with our pants down but you did mighty good. Afraid you've lost Major Hartmann, though — the first bullet got him.'

There were six dead and eight wounded among the Confederates. Winters made sure they were getting attention and went to his own sergeant, O'Malley.

'How did we do, Paddy?'

'Chadwick's gone, sir, an' I'm thinkin' young Harris will soon be jinin' him. They was good pals in life, sir. Nice to think they — might — you know. Meet again.'

'How many wounded, Sergeant?' Brad asked.

'Three more, sir — no ... four.' O'Malley suddenly scratched his head. 'That can't be right — must be one of the Major's patrol. Our men're all accounted for ... '

'Get it sorted out. I'll need exact figures for my report.'

The burly sergeant gave a half salute and Winters moved on, kneeling beside some of the wounded and exchanging a few comforting words. He checked the new guards and, satisfied, was walking back towards the rebuilt fire, sheltered within boulders this time, when O'Malley came up, panting.

'That — that wounded Reb, sir, the one we wasn't sure was ours . . .'

'And is he ours, O'Malley?'

'No, sir — seems he belongs to the major's patrol. Likely the scout they were sent to find they think.'

'The hell're you talking about? Don't they know their own man?'

O'Malley swallowed. 'He's wearing Confederate uniform, sir — or what's left of it. Some of it's been slashed up and burned. Stiff with blood. *Dried* blood. And he looks like — well, like the Injuns've been at him. He's startin' to come round an' if he is who they think, his name is Ryan . . .'

Winters, starting forward, paused. 'Ryan?'

'That's what he says, sir,' O'Malley said slowly, looking strangely at the officer. 'Would you be knowin' someone by that name at all . . . ?'

'It's a common enough name, Sergeant. Lead on,' Winters snapped and in a few moments he saw the small group gathered around the odd man out who was lying on a blanket.

He was young; they could see that even through the blood and dirt and burns and other wounds. One of Hartmann's men held a flaming torch where it threw plenty of light on the maimed body. A couple of fingers had been hacked off. Toenails had been torn out by their roots, likely with a pair of pliers. The young body bore horrific scars, from groin to scalp.

'By God, he must be a tough wee bugger, sir,' O'Malley said with some admiration in his voice. 'Indians've been at him. Mebbe he escaped, got to our camp an' that's why they attacked, comin' in to take him back?'

Winters snapped his head up. 'That's

37

a good theory, O'Malley. I'd say likely the right one . . . '

'N-no . . . ' the tortured man grated, startling them all. 'Not In-Indians — '

'Jesus, Mary an' Joseph!' exclaimed O'Malley huskily. 'Then, who did this to you, boy?'

'Y-Yankees.' The effort was too much and he slumped, though still breathing heavily and raggedly.

There was a stunned silence and Winters knelt, took a water-soaked cloth from one of the troopers and wiped the boy's face gently. They all heard the inward hissing of his breath, the hushed, 'Good God Almighty!'

'You know him, sir?'

Brad Winters didn't answer at first, then nodded slowly. 'Yes . . . I know him . . . '

* * *

As in the past, he awoke, with a cry of anguish choking him, rasping his throat, sweat-drenched, his big body shaking, fighting for breath.

He sucked down enough air to mumble, 'Oh, Ryan, boy! Why didn't you stay on the ranch, helping out Ma and Pa? Why the hell did you have to follow me to war?'

3

New Arrivals

'You look like hell this morning, Brad, old pard.'

Winters turned from the bowl of grey water at the washbench, ravaged-looking face dripping, and grabbed the rag of a towel, mopping-up. He only grunted at Farrell's remark.

The rancher pursed his lips, stroking his clean-shaven jaw lightly. 'Well, I know you haven't been to town, and the only liquor on the spread is locked up in that big cupboard in my office — or better be! But you sure look like you've raised a couple of roofs somewhere — or maybe a couple of skirts?'

Winters didn't seem amused, flung the now sodden towel heavily into the bowl, splashing water on his shirt. He swore.

'Man, you are in a *mood!*' grinned the rancher.

'Had a bad night is all — too tired to sleep.'

'Well, I told you you work too hard — ' Farrell broke off and sobered. 'Oh-oh. Now I know what's happened. You've had that nightmare again, after all this time, haven't you?'

Winters' eyes were bleak. 'Told you I didn't sleep well.'

'I'm sorry, Brad. Wasn't thinking. Of course, the show we're arranging has brought it all back, hasn't it?' Matt snapped his fingers. 'No! It was that name *Endicott!* You know, you've told me that story of finding your kid brother at the Pincushion, but I don't believe you ever went beyond that point. Like, what happened afterwards.'

'Nothing much more to tell. Ryan had lied about his age to join up — hoped to catch up with me somewhere in the war. Tell you how naïve he was: he used the name of Adam Ryan, Adam being Ma's maiden name. We had an uncle, Bradford, the one I'm named for. He lived in the mountains, the Big Smokies, and Ryan spent a deal of time with him. A good deal.'

'Not you?'

Brad shook his head. 'I was big and strong by then, more use on the ranch, but Ryan learnt a lot of wilderness stuff from Unk Bradford, put it to use when he joined the army. They sent him in to scout the Yankees near Pincushion and he was caught. Seems he heard or saw something he shouldn't've: they'd stolen a Confederate hospital train, killed all on board, crew, wounded rebs, everyone — and were planning to use it to ship ammo and supplies to the new fort they were setting up on the *Llano*.'

They had walked across the yard now, towards the covered dog-run where the crew were noisily at breakfast. Both slowed so they wouldn't reach the tables before Brad finished speaking.

'Ryan escaped the Yankees after they

tortured him, literally crawled back to Hartmann's camp just as the raid started. He lived long enough to tell us they wanted to find out if he'd had anyone with him when he spied on them, or had managed to get a message away. The Yankee in charge, the one who ordered the torture, was a Colonel Kel Endicott.'

Matt Farrell pursed his lips. 'How come you never told me any of this before?'

Winters shrugged. 'Trying to forget, I guess. Didn't count on the dreams coming back, though.'

Matt nodded, touching Brad lightly on the arm. 'I'm a thoughtless son of a bitch at times. Sorry, Brad, let's go eat.'

Brad Winters didn't move. Matt turned back towards him, arching his eyebrows. 'After we buried Ryan, I kept it to myself, what he'd told me. My troop was on independent orders at the time. War was going badly for the South; my job was to harass the hell out of the Yankees any way I could. Ryan told me when they were gonna use that train, still set up like a hospital unit, to transport ammunition and supplies to the *Llano* fort. They had to cross Deacon's Drop and the only way over was by the high trestle bridge.'

Matt suddenly grinned. 'By hell, I remember that part now! Free-ranging Reb company dynamited the bridge when the train was in the middle — blew everything to hell-and-gone, even widened the gorge when the banks collapsed! They say you could hear the explosion ten miles away!'

'She was a big one all right,' Brad admitted, with a faint smile of remembrance. 'I'd always believed that Colonel Kel Endicott was on board — until Joe Briscoe told me different yesterday.'

Sober-faced, Matt nodded. 'Now Endicott's gonna show up here at Hashknife Ridge.'

Winters' eyes were as merciless as a snake's as he said quietly, 'I sure as hell hope so, Matt — I sure as hell hope so.'

★ ★ ★

44

Originally, the town was called Hash-knife Ridge, too, but as it was the same name as the small mountain outside of town, it caused a good deal of confusion. So the town name was simply shortened to Hashknife.

It was a sprawling town, pretty much the usual kind in that part of the cattle country. The streets were wide and meandering in most cases, although a couple along the river bank behind the town proper were little better than trails — and mostly avoided by locals after dark.

There was a large business section, three blocks long, with a variety of goods and services on offer. The red light district was only one short, dead-end street running off the southern end of Main. There were two pleasure houses, but only one counted, the biggest and brightest called The Comet. The entrance was through a big arched gateway painted with a garish swinging signboard carrying a rendition of a shooting star — with a barely clad, nubile laughing woman riding the top point. The other bordello was a second-rate affair but had its customers: its prices were well below those of the Comet. So was their standard of service. And gals.

There was one large saloon, called Mooney's, and a few bars that were little more than trestles set up on empty beer kegs under canvas. They all managed to make a living when the railroad pens were full of cattle and the trail men had pay-day dollars burning holes in their pockets.

The bank was a two-storey adobe and brick affair with bars on all the windows, except the big street-front one — though this, too, was boarded-up securely during the winter storm season — or the other 'storms', more frequent, when the cowboys lifted the lid to see what made Hashknife tick.

The law office and jail was twice as big as that in most Western towns, which surprised a lot of folk, but this was a prosperous town and not all that far from Indian Territory — the Cherokee Strip. Now and again some of the wild boys who lived there and had their pictures on wanted dodgers decided to try and relieve the town of some of its riches. Sheriff Slade Samson saw to it that they were given his best accommodation while they waited for interested lawmen from all over the country to come and collect them. Those who didn't have enough sense to throw down their guns when ordered, Slade buried in the neatly kept Boot Hill on the rise above the river. Quite a picturesque spot for a man's last resting-place.

It was one of the few things that didn't appeal to Mort Tibbetts and his sidekick, Griffin, when they rode into Hashknife one Wednesday after-noon.

'Like the bank, though,' Tibbetts told Griffin who rode alongside him, slumped easily in the saddle.

Griffin was a slab-bodied man,

medium tall, but his short legs were like tree-trunks and bulged his worn Levis.

'Banker's family might live upstairs,' he opined.

'I would love that, Griff. I surely would!'

Tibbetts, rangy and straight in his Mexican saddle, winked. He had a narrow face and you could easily mistake him for a friendly type — until you noticed those small, close together eyes and realized that, although his thin lips might be smiling, there was no true warmth in the way he looked at a man. He had a reckless cast to him but that was misleading, too. Mort Tibbetts was a man who planned carefully in every move he made. '*In-born Yankee thoroughness*,' he liked to say.

Griffin turned his coarse-looking face towards his sidekick now and thick, leathery lips peeled back from surprisingly even, though tobacco-stained, teeth. 'You workin' on it already?'

Tibbetts grinned. 'Been workin' on it since we first heard about this Remembrance Day, month or so back.'

Griffin frowned. 'But we never been here before. You dunno nothin' about the place.'

'Which is why we are here now. Judd and the others'll drift in from t'other end of town and when we meet up we'll compare notes . . . Better than comin' in in a bunch and ridin' through checkin' out the place. This Samson's one tough sheriff. He killed Monte Dangerfield in Wichita, a while back.'

'Was that him?' Griffin blew out his stubbled cheeks. 'Hell, mebbe this town'll be too much for us, Mort.'

Tibbetts scoffed. 'Ain't seen any Reb town that's too much for me. Gimme a few days and I'll have all the details worked out.'

'But what fazes me, Mort, is we dunno there'll be a worthwhile bunch of loot. We're just hopin'.'

'You're just hopin': I'm plannin'.

Stick with me, Griff, and I'll make you rich, feller. Guarantee it.'

'Hell, never had no notion of not stickin', Mort.'

'Let's go take a look at Mooney's, and keep your ears cocked. We can pick up a lot in a bar big as that one.'

* * *

From inside his office, sitting in a comfortable chair back from the big street window, Sheriff Slade Samson lowered the field-glasses he had had trained on Tibbetts and Griffin — and every other stranger who had ridden into town from that direction over the last few days.

He grunted, a big man, neatly dressed, and with a single Colt in the holster on the bullet belt that slanted across a more-than-ample belly. He reached out to a small table beside his chair and lifted a notepad and stub of pencil. He wrote briefly.

Two men. Tall one riding a palomino. Looks too good for his kind. Other on grulla with white ear tip. Check dodgers. They have the Look.

Anyone seeing this would find the word 'sneaky' dropping into their mind, and they would be right. Slade Samson did resort to sneaky tactics. But he was often up-front, too, and they were the times that counted with the townsfolk, when his six-gun bounced off the skull of some loud-mouthed drunk, or a couple of brawling cowpokes. Or, a few times, that same gun had roared and cut down the odd fool who figured he could out-draw a big-bellied fat man who walked with a slight limp.

Far as the town was concerned, Sheriff Slade Samson could keep the law any way he wanted in Hashknife, because he made it a safe place to live. And if anyone could keep it that way through the expected high-jinks of Remembrance Day and associated celebrations, it was Slade Samson and his well-trained deputies.

★ ★ ★

Reed Galvin knew the deal and how things operated. He was the new boy in town, the gambler here for the quick kill, and the locals would, naturally, resent him. It had happened a few times in other towns and once he had spent seven weeks in some railroad town infirmary, recovering from a busted leg and broken hand. Another time he had lost some teeth — it required a visit to St Louis and most of his money to have them fixed — and once he had been shot.

But he had killed the man who put the bullet in his side. It had been a fair shoot-out and no one had ever pushed the accusation made by the man, now dead, that Reed had dealt from the bottom of the deck. He packed a short-barrelled Sheriff's Model Colt in .44 calibre. Heavy to carry but compact enough and he had had a special underarm holster made: it gripped the cylinder tightly enough so he could hang the gun upside down. This way he saved precious seconds being able to close his hand over the butt and trigger the moment gunplay became inevitable.

He shed his frock coat and rolled it up in his warbag, slipping on an ankle-length dust coat that was becoming popular with travellers in the dusty areas these days. He went into Mooney's, spent some time at the bar, buying the 'keep two drinks, and learning the saloon was owned by a man called Trimble. Without actually asking, he learned it would be wise for any new gambler coming to town to have a meeting with Trimble before dealing his first card.

For a silver dollar, the barkeep arranged it.

The meeting was upstairs in Trimble's office. The saloon man was in his mid-fifties, weary, bags under his eyes and a stare that was neither hostile nor welcoming. He had big blunt hands and toyed with an ivory cigar holder as he looked over this new arrival.

Reed Galvin was tall, straight-backed, square-shouldered and had added to his disarming charm with a pencil moustache above his ready-to-smile mouth. He removed his hat carefully so it didn't disturb his pomaded, wavy dark hair.

'Don't care for pretty boys,' Trimble said, and there was a slight movement in the shadows beyond the saloon man.

Galvin tensed, noticing a silent man leaning against the wall beyond the lights, arms folded, twin guns on his hips. He couldn't make out the man's face, but that wasn't too important. He flashed a half smile at the saloon man.

'My looks help my profession, Mr Trimble: got an honest face. But I admit they've been — er — altered now and again, before I realized it was wise to confer with the owner of the biggest saloon in town before I dealt my first card.'

Trimble snorted. 'This is the *only* saloon in town, mister. Them little piss-ant bars don't count . . . What's your name and what d'you want?'

'Reed Galvin, and I want in on your gambling concession. I'm a card man, but I've handled roulette, keno, faro, any dice game you care to name.'

Trimble's big right hand waved all that away. 'Wouldn't expect you to say any different. How about your winnin's? Good or bad?'

Galvin strained to have that charming smile work but he felt it wasn't going to be too successful. 'I believe I can make both of us an attractive income, Mr Trimble.'

'Twenty-five per cent goes to the house.' Trimble jerked a thick thumb against his chest.

Reed blew out his cheeks. 'Well, now, that's bordering on the outrageous!'

'No negotiation.' Trimble flicked his gaze towards the man in the shadows. 'Mr Meeker, I believe our friend here is ready to leave.'

Meeker stepped out, medium tall, long-faced with a bitter mouth. He started forward, hands resting on his gun butts. Galvin stood slowly.

'Now wait a minute! I-I never said I wouldn't agree to what you're asking.'

'Never said you would, either. OK, Meek, ease up a little.'

Galvin was breathing harder than he wanted to, kept looking at Meeker as he turned back to Trimble. 'What do I get for my twenty-five per cent?'

'Protection.' Trimble gestured to Meeker again. 'A free chance at any of the saloon girls who're interested, once a night — cut-rate booze, for yourself. You buy for the players, you pay bar-rates.'

'You are cutting yourself a good deal, here, Mr Trimble.' It annoyed Galvin that sweat was sheening his face.

The saloon man shrugged heavy shoulders. 'You can have a room but you'll have to share. Gonna be kinda crowded when all them visitors arrive, so might even have to turn you out to accommodate payin' customers. Now, that's enough for you to think about — what d'you say?'

Galvin was shaking a little as he nodded and said, hoarsely, 'I agree.'

'OK. Meek'll show you where you can sleep. Stable your horse at the livery.'

'I came by train.'

'See? You're already saving money. Speakin' of which, I need a bond.'

'Bond?' Galvin blinked.

'Yeah, in case you lose more'n you got in your pockets. Couple of hundred'll do . . . to start.'

Reed Galvin sighed, reached for his wallet. He knew he'd never see one cent of that bond money again.

By God, he was going to have to work hard to make any real money in this dump!

Work hard, or shuffle hard . . . *and fast!*

4

Crowds

Sheriff Slade Samson sent out his deputies, then grabbed Boney Carson, a local wild youth in his usual patched bib-and-brace overalls, the trouser legs of which barely covered his shins, as he was sidling past on the boardwalk, hoping to slip past unnoticed.

'Where you off to, Boney, lookin' so sly?'

'Aw, gee, Sher'ff! Lemme go — I ain't done nothin'. I dunno nothin' about them Epsom salts in the Dowd Street hoss-trough, honest!'

Samson straightened. 'Funny thing, Boney, I din' know anythin' about it neither — till you just told me.'

'Awwwww — geez!' Boney doubled over as if *he* had been drinking at the horse trough. Boney never was too

58

bright and the sheriff shook him roughly.

'You damn kids! Think it's funny, eh? Hosses shittin' all over the place with all these visitors in town! Well, I know the bunch you run with an' I'll haul in every last one and kick their asses till their noses bleed!' He shook the terrified boy some more. 'Yours, too. Then you're all gonna clean the streets and walks and wherever else they crap, hear? Don't worry — I'll make sure they know who squealed on 'em, too.'

'I didn't mean to! They — they'll kill me!'

'Paint your privates with tar, more like. OK. You go find the fellers whose names are writ on this paper and tell 'em to report to my office pronto for deputy duty. You do that in half an hour and I'll let you off and keep mum about you tellin'.'

Boney couldn't believe his ears. 'But wh-what about after?'

'After's your problem, if they figure it out, well, I was you I'd go hide someplace. Specially if that Frog Delaney's in on it.'

Boney sagged more, whining. 'Was Frog's idea.'

The sheriff placed his hands on his hips. 'That don't surprise me; now get goin', boy, before I change my mind!'

Boney scooted, stumbling the first few yards, and Samson smothered a laugh. 'Damn kids!' he muttered but with a grudging admiration. 'What a notion! Some of them snooty old maids'll have a purple fit when the hosses start.'

He chuckled and shook his head as he walked away down the street, big shoulders shaking with his mirth. Folk stared — Samson wasn't a man anyone associated with levity.

Limping his way towards Dowd Street, the sheriff lost all humour as he crossed Main, aiming for the corner. He saw two riders turning in towards the red light district and stopped dead.

'By God! I know that one!' He spoke half aloud but people on the walks didn't take any real notice. Not until he stepped directly into the path of the horsemen, right hand resting on his gun butt, left raised in the 'halt' sign.

'Hold it, you two! Where the hell you think you're goin'?'

Both men hauled rein, yanking their mounts' heads up, the smoke whinnying a little. The grey rolled its eyes, nostrils quivering, ready to run if nudged by the spurs. Its rider was an ordinary-looking cowpoke, medium build, face a mite rugged but friendly, untidy brown hair with a few silver tips poking out from under his weathered hat. He swivelled his gaze from the lawman to his partner.

This man was more rawboned, and he had a cast in his left eye which blinked rapidly when he saw the sheriff. His nose twitched from side to side as he said, 'Hell almighty! Samson! I never 'spected to see you!'

'That I believe, Judd. Now be a good feller and toss me down your gun.' Without taking his eyes off Judd,

61

Samson added, 'An' tell your pard he'd be wise to hand over his Colt, too.'

'I ain't no pard of his!' said the friendly looking rider quickly, easing his mount back. 'We . . . we just met crossin' the bridge. Was gonna have a drink together — company, you know?'

Still watching Judd, Samson growled, 'You oughta be more careful who you talk to, mister. Just toss me your Colt anyway.'

Someone yelled 'Gun!' on the walk and the gathering crowd suddenly scattered in a dozen different directions. Men on the street itself ducked for cover and riders hauled rein and spurred aside quickly.

Judd had gone for his gun while the lawman was diverted, talking to the friendly looking man.

Judd's Colt was almost clear of leather when Samson's gun blasted through the afternoon. The gunman was lifted to his toes in the stirrups but he threw down with his pistol and fired even as a passing rider swung his horse towards the boardwalk, yelling, 'Watch it, Sheriff!'

It was Brad Winters, and he palmed up his gun, firing two fast shots hard on the heels of the lawman's Colt, as the second man brought up his six-gun, shooting wild. This man suddenly spun out of the saddle, his hat sailing wildly across the boardwalk, head snapping back as he spilled untidily and lay on his side in the dust.

Slade Samson had dropped to one knee, sagging to his right, hand still holding his smoking Colt as he pressed it into a bleeding wound in his side.

Brad Winters quit his saddle, glanced towards the sheriff. 'How you doin', Slade? You need the sawbones or the undertaker?'

'I'm a long way from needin' a goddamned undertaker,' gasped the sheriff, fighting up to both feet again. He swayed and set a cold gaze on the ramrod. 'My job ain't up for grabs yet a spell!'

Winters nodded. 'Glad to hear it.

That second feller nearly got you. Know 'em?' He watched the man he had shot closely.

'The one I nailed was Judd McCoy. Man's a damn fool showin' his face around here. I told him last time I'd shoot him on sight if he ever showed his nose in my town again.'

'Well, you always was a man of your word, Slade.' Brad shook his head, looking down at the dead man. 'He was a blamed fool all right. Either that or he had some damn good reason for takin' the chance of drawing on you.'

Samson snapped his head up, frowned, then studied the wound in his side: he had had worse. He looked hard at the second man, thought the mouth twitched. 'He still breathin'?'

'Know him, too?' asked Winters, nodding.

'Think it's Hal McVeeters. I seen him workin' up around Walsenburg, out at the Triple J, while back. They lost some steers and he disappeared about the same time.'

'Yeah, nearly hired him once on Block F. Looks like I creased his skull. My Colt must be pullin' high and to the left again, goddamnit.'

'Well, get it fixed before we get too many more from the Cherokee Strip comin' into town.' Samson had his neckerchief pressed against his wound now. 'Next time you mightn't just wing one of them Yankees in the arm if it ain't shootin' straight.'

The sheriff locked gazes with Winters who shucked out the used shells and thumbed home new ones from his belt. He smiled crookedly. 'Glad I happened along, Slade.'

Samson flushed a little as Ty Carver, one of his deputies came running up, hot and bothered. 'I heard shootin'.'

'You shoulda been doin' some of it.' Samson gestured to McVeeters who was sitting up groggily now, holding his bleeding head. 'Take him down to the office and keep him there till I get back from the sawbones — and get that corpse outa sight.'

The deputy nodded, took the groggy McVeeters by the arm and called sharply to the crowd to make way, half-dragging the wounded man. The sheriff watched Brad Winters mounting again.

'Glad you happened along, too, Brad.' He was breathing heavily now, the neckerchief covering his wound already sodden with blood. 'Din' mean to be so tetchy . . . you wanna use live ammo on them Yankees, I won't see nor hear a thing.'

He hawked and Winters smiled again. 'Think I better stick to blanks, Slade. *Adios.*'

He heeled his mount forward and angled across towards Halstrom's General store.

'You ever quit Farrell, I'll make a deputy's place for you,' the sheriff called, but Winters made no sign that he had heard.

★ ★ ★

Across the street and down a little, leaning on the rails of the gate to the livery's corrals, Mort Tibbett mashed his cigarette butt into the wood savagely and swore. Griffin was beside him and grunted,

'Short a couple of men now, Mort.'

'You don't say! You smart enough to figure that out all by yourself?' Griffin flushed but held his tongue. 'Damn that Samson. Got eyes like a hawk. You an' me better stay off the streets.'

Griffin grinned with his broken teeth. 'Where you wanna hang out? Mooney's or Bucktooth Bertha's?'

Tibbetts scowled. 'You won't think it's funny tryin' to do the job without Judd's gun to back us.'

Griffin's smile slowly faded. 'Bigger share for the rest of us, Mort, think of it that way.'

Tibbetts gave him a withering look, spat and watched Brad Winters dismounting at the hitch rail outside the store.

'Remember that ranny, Griff.'

Griffin nodded, hurried after him as he turned and walked away. 'What about Hal?'

Tibbetts slowed and turned smouldering eyes on Griffin. 'We have to hope he don't talk.'

Griffin merely nodded. 'Hal won't hold out for long.'

'This time he better. You might have to get yourself arrested — to make sure.'

The idea didn't seem to appeal to Griffin.

★   ★   ★

Bede Halstrom had a head of colourless hair, neither blond nor wheat-coloured nor silver-grey. It was a kind of negative mix of all those and he sure had a mop of it. Now he grinned with his big teeth, overshadowed by the large hooked nose, lifted a meaty hand and pushed some of the hair back off his forehead.

'Ah, I haff been expectin' you or the good Mr Farrell to show up, Bradley.

You are bringing the signed authority?'

He looked at the folded paper Winters was holding and the ramrod nodded, spread the square of paper on top of the scarred counter. He tapped it once.

'All there, Bede. All the ammo listed, the star shells, fireworks, blank cartridges, percussion caps, powder-packs for the cannon, slow matches, fuses. Be here on tomorrow's train with a bunch of spare uniforms. Matt says you're donating a box of dynamite . . . ?'

'Yerz, yerz, that I am doing.' Halstrom scanned the list, adjusting his half-moon spectacles, lips moving as he ran his finger down the hand-written list. 'My Piers vas lost in the Hashknife fight, you must be knowing.'

Brad Winters nodded. 'Never knew your son, Bede, but I've heard a lot about him. All good.'

Halstrom sighed as he nodded. 'Yerz, a good boy he was being and would haff made a fine man if he had been allowed to grow up.' He lifted his eyes towards the roof where hides and shackles and harness dangled from the rafters. 'But it vas the Lord's vish to call him to His side so ve haff to live with it.' He shook the paper Brad had given him. 'This I vill be showing to the army and vill be stowing in my rooms at back. I haff one lined with sheet metal for long time now and I haff new padlocks and chains. It vill all be safe until the battle day.'

'Yeah. Matt's arranging with Emmett Barlow to store the weapons in his freight warehouse.' He handed across another tightly folded paper. 'Some goods I'll pick up later to take back to Block F — then I might be able to get on with some ranch work instead of traipsing all over the county making arrangements for this damn Battle Day — that's what they're calling it now instead of Remembrance day. Oh, and gimme a couple sacks of Bull Durham and some papers, Bede.' Brad counted out some coins and put the tobacco in his shirt pockets.

'You are shooting outside I hear, Bradley.'

Winters nodded. 'Couple of hard-cases Slade recognized from the Strip. He had to draw and shoot one. The other tried to gun him in the back.'

'But you are stopping him, eh?' Halstrom shook his head ponderously. 'This Battle Day — bring good money for everyone, but I think it be bringing some trouble too, Bradley.'

'Well, where you got a lot of people crowded together, bound to find a few who like to act-up.'

'Yerz. I haff some boards for my vindows made. I vill be putting them up each night until it is all over.'

'Good idea, Bede.' Brad touched fingers to his hat brim and went out.

He paused to roll and light a cigarette, watching the crowds shuffling along the street, wagons rolling; some newcomers, lost and making the wrong turn into streets, causing chaos and arguments. He had been in Cripple Creek during the gold rush and it wasn't much different to this. In a way, this was a gold rush, too: plenty of people were coming purely for the entertainment, but there were lots of others who had their eye out for the fast buck and the easy dollar. And everyone was spending one way and another.

He lit the cigarette and tossed the used match away. He wasn't a man who cared much for crowds, especially jostling, impatient ones, single-mindedly shoving their way around with neither care nor manners, eyes fastened on that next dollar that had a home waiting for it in their pockets.

He glanced towards Mooney's: should he forget about a drink and head on back to the ranch? *Hell no!* Why forego the pleasure of a couple of cold beers just because the town was filling up with a lot of boisterous idiots?

He pushed through the batwings, blinked at the jam-packed crowds but was carried forward into the crush by other men coming in behind. It was all jostling and cursing and some savage insults were flung about when drinks were spilled, but there were no real fights — yet. Brad, regretting his decision to enter, eventually found himself up against the bar and signalled to the 'keep for two beers.

The sweating man slapped the two foaming, slopping glasses on the wet counter top and picked up Winters' money after several tries. Brad drank.

'This is warm, Burt!' he complained, and the harassed barkeep snarled at him.

'Then tell the bastards not to drink so fast! Ice is meltin' faster'n we can replace it. It's take it or leave it day, Brad.'

Winters nodded, swilled some more tepid beer and decided he could do without the other. He tapped the arm of the man next to him.

'Friend, you've just earned yourself a free beer.' He thrust the second glass at the man and it slopped onto the grimy shirt sleeve.

'Goddammit, what the hell you

comin' at?' *A Yankee accent and not friendly.*

Surprised, Brad shrugged. 'Beer's not to my liking — thought you might care for it.'

'Ah! Gettin' rid of your reb pigswill on me, huh!'

'Mister, just trying to be friendly. You don't want it, toss it away — I don't care one way or t'other.'

Winters turned and started to thrust his way back through the crush — and suddenly felt the beer poured over his hat and down the back of his shirt.

There was a sudden silence rippling through the room at this direct challenge and somehow men backed up and cleared a space that left Brad Winters, dripping foamy beer, facing the ungrateful stranger who, it seemed, would rather pick a fight than accept a free beer. He didn't know the man's name was Griffin, and that the Northerner had already taken rotgut whiskey and a lot of beer on board. Not that it really mattered: Griffin was spoiling for a fight and shook off the restraining hand of Mort Tibbetts, concentrating on Winters.

Brad blinked away some beer that had seeped through his hat and pulled out a kerchief to wipe his face. The man still facing him with the empty beer mug in his hand, curled a lip. 'White kerchief for surrender, huh? Typical reb!'

Then Winters flung the neckerchief at the man and it fluttered like a bird in front of Griffin's face.

Although it couldn't cause him any harm, Griffin instinctively stepped back, wrenching his head aside to dodge the cloth. There was a big fist waiting and it smashed into his face, sending him stumbling back into the crowd, fighting to keep his balance. He staggered against Mort Tibbetts, who pushed him away quickly, adding strength to the move so that Griffin cannoned into Winters as the ramrod followed through.

Not expecting to meet Griffin so quickly, Brad mistimed his blow and it had no sting when it skimmed across Griffin's ear. But the Yankee roared as if he had been goosed by a hot poker and came in with a long, lifting stride, swinging the heavy beer glass by its handle. It would have spilled the cowman's brains in the sawdust if Brad hadn't weaved and twisted. The glass bounced off his left shoulder tip and staggered him.

Griffin hurled the glass but Winters moved his head aside and someone in the cheering crowd shouted. Griffin followed the glass forward, big fists sledging wildly. Brad covered as best he could but there wasn't enough space for manoeuvring. He stopped two solid blows that brought him up short and Griffin rammed a knee up towards his groin. Brad took it on his thigh but was knocked off-balance.

Down amongst the tangling feet of the surging crowd, the cowman rolled and slammed a few shins so as to make room. Then he twisted onto all fours and came up as if hurled by a spring.

Griffin was bulling his way in, slugging and chopping. Winters took some of the blows on his forearms, felt them throbbing and jarring as he covered, then ducked under a whistling left, straightened abruptly, and drove the top of his head into the middle of Griffin's face.

Nose and lips crushed, and Brad felt the man's front teeth butt against his forehead, splitting the skin. Blood flowed. But it gushed from Griffin's nose and his eyes were actually crossed briefly as he staggered like a drunk looking for the privy in the dark.

Winters stepped in, shaking his aching, sore hands, knuckles feeling crushed. He needed those hands working and supple for the ranch. So, to save them a little he closed with Griffin and drove an elbow down onto the top of the man's head after hooking him in the midriff.

Griffin's legs seemed to go out from under him and in an instant he was on his knees, dazed, wondering what had happened. Brad lifted a knee to the side of the man's head, sent him sprawling in the sawdust. He rolled slowly onto his side, gagging, spitting blood and broken teeth.

Gasping, chest heaving, Brad stepped back, needing the pause as much as Griffin. But he had under-estimated the other man: Griffin spun suddenly and came up as if a cougar was on his tail. Winters just managed to get his guard up but stumbled when he took the main force of the blow on his left forearm. He instinctively lifted and was surprised when he realized Griffin's right arm was on top of his arm. So it rose with Brad's left — and there was Griffin's bloody face and upper chest all exposed without protection.

Winters jabbed with his right, one — two — three — four, rapping Griffin's head back with each blow, blood spraying as the Yankee fought to stay on his feet. The cowman closed, braced his legs and hammered a volley of lightning-like blows into Griffin's midriff and chest. The man was out on his feet before Brad straight-armed him with a left, measuring, an instant before his right followed, shoulder and body behind it, the fist turning as it smeared Griffin's already mangled face.

The man went down and took four of the crowd with him. They scrambled to their feet, swearing, but Griffin stayed there on the blood-spattered sawdust.

Someone with a sense of humour, poured a glass of warm beer over the man, saying, 'Have that reb beer after all, friend!' But Griffin was too far gone to come round just yet.

Moving his feet constantly so as to keep his balance, Winters mopped at his face and bleeding lower lip, feeling one eye closing.

Then he was aware of the man who had shoved Griffin back at him earlier, standing right in front of him, hand on gun butt. Tibbetts lifted his free hand and poked a stiffened forefinger into Winters' chest.

'That's twice today you've put

friends of mine out of action, feller.'
The finger began to jab, emphasizing
each word as he added, 'There
. . . won't . . . be . . . a . . . third
. . . time — savvy?'

Tibbetts didn't wait for an answer.
He turned away sharply and kicked the
moaning Griffin in the side before
stepping over him and fighting his way
towards the batwings.

Burt shouldered his way through the
jabbering men and offered Winters a
bar towel wrapped about something
that dripped and crackled.

'Last of the ice, Brad. Reckon you've
earned it.'

Winters took the pack and made a
small moaning sound of pleasure as he
held its coldness against his battered
face.

5

Gathering

'I think I'd better ride in alone to see Emmett,' Matt Farrell said, tugging at his riding gloves on the porch of the sprawling ranch house. 'Trouble seems to ambush you lately, Brad.'

Standing with one boot on the bottom step, Winters half-smiled and immediately winced as his swollen bottom lip began to bleed a little. 'Suits me. There's plenty to do out on the range.'

Farrell's look was sharp. 'Yes — Monkey said you wanted to see me before I leave.'

'Yeah, that feller who told me I'd 'put two of his friends out of action' is named Mort Tibbetts. Slade Samson says he's well known in the Cherokee Strip but he doesn't have any dodgers

81

on him. I wondered about the two friends he mentioned. I'd just had the fight with Griffin but only other thing I did was shoot that ranny who tried to kill Samson — McVeeters. Which seems to tie him in with Tibbetts.'

'You tell Slade?'

'He already had it figured — says he's gonna question McVeeters. Might be something going on, he thinks, with known hardcases drifting in separately, like they don't want to be linked together.'

Farrell frowned. 'Hell, I hope not! But there's bound to be someone looking to make an easy dollar out of all this. I'll check with Slade when I get into town. You heading out to Hashknife Ridge?'

'Yeah. Kit tells me the campers are moving in already, but you said to leave 'em be.'

'Hell, yeah, Brad. No point in giving them a hard time. Let 'em settle in their place to watch. Some of the 'soldiers' are setting-up, too. I'm not going to follow history exactly: in the original battle, our boys were lined up clear across the valley and had some emplacements on the ridge slopes . . . I'm trying to keep it all down in the flats.'

'That wasn't how it was?'

Matt shook his head. 'No. Both cannon were up on the ridge top facing to the south. Might put one up there, align it more north towards where the Yankees'll ride in. It'll give good coverage and look more spectacular when they shoot those fireworks shells. They're six-pounders. Make a big bang.'

Winters rubbed his bruised and cut forehead gently. 'I'm not too keen on those damn cannon, Matt.'

'It'll be mighty spectacular, Brad! Use your imagination. Kids'll love it — their parents, too, I reckon.'

'Matt, I'm using my know-how, not my imagination. Fireworks are prime spookers for cattle and we'll have herds spread all around there. It only takes a handful of sparks to waft across on the breeze and we could have a stampede that won't stop this side of Denver. Then there's the horses . . . '

'I've thought of that: if the wind's blowing the wrong way, we'll just turn the cannon in the other direction, run the horses back into the canyons for fireworks night. This is *entertainment*, Brad, pure and simple. Do it well, and we can make it an annual event.'

Winters scowled. 'Won't that be something to look forward to!'

Farrell's eyes narrowed. 'Well, this is the way I'm going to do it, Brad. I have the backing of the town and the Cattlemen's Alliance. We'll really put Hashknife on the map. Don't be so goddamn stuffy — and tell Dan and Beesting to rig up a buckboard and come with me. Might as well unload and stow the prop guns while we're in town.'

'*Prop* guns? What the hell're they?'

Farrell smiled, knowingly. 'See? You are behind the times. 'Prop' is short for 'property'. A stage term, they tell me, for all the items they use in a show: clocks, chairs, coffee jugs, that sort of thing. They call 'em all 'props'.'

'Thought these were real guns, genuine muzzle-loaders from the war with a coupla Spencers and Henrys thrown in?'

Matt sighed. 'They're real. They'll shoot real bullets if you load 'em, but they're out of date now. Mostly find 'em hung on someone's wall as a souvenir or in museums. I was lucky to track down this lot: old army stock in good condition. I'll sell 'em to collectors afterwards.'

Winters was losing interest. Matt Farrell had always been used to money, and enjoyed making it. His family's plantation and estate had been razed by the Yankees back in his home state of Georgia. But he turned up here with enough cash to buy Block F and to expand, and hadn't stopped chasing the dollars since.

He experimented with different seed bulls over the years, lifted the quality of his herds and claimed he had the best beefsteaks in the country walking around Hashknife County. He gambled with some stocks and shares, but that didn't work out. Undeterred, he plunged on railroad stock and apparently called in a few favours owed him by a senator he knew and had the tracks run to Hashknife instead of skirting the valley and going to Alamosa as originally planned.

Naturally, he was looked on as Hashknife's mentor and saviour, for bringing in the railroad had put the town on the beef-market map, attracting herds and meathouse agents from all over. It must have been easy for him to persuade the town council and the Cattlemen's Alliance to back the staging of this Battle Day: seemed he could do no wrong.

A lot of folk were going to get rich it appeared, but Brad Winters figured he wouldn't be one of them.

All it meant to him was one damn big headache.

Then he realized just how smart Farrell was: Winters would be the unpopular one and have to bear the hostility and complaints, while Matt wined and dined his special guests and generally made a good fellow of himself. Brad Winters felt the black mood growing on him with this realization. What made it harder to swallow, was that this wasn't Farrell's usual behaviour. He could be hard and rough-tongued when he wanted his own way, but he was usually fair.

And in Brad's opinion this *wasn't* fair.

★ ★ ★

It probably coloured Winters' attitude when he took Kit Turner and Spud Bromley with him on an inspection of the ridge area. He wanted to get the lay of the land and had a rough sketch map Matt had given him, outlining the general areas for spectators and the camps of the opposing forces.

Brad didn't agree with any of it, although the spectator section was outside of the ranch's working area. He aimed to police it as best he could without starting a real battle. As he led the two riders in through the narrow pass, he could hear the lowing of grazing cattle over the ridge and further back upstream on the river pastures. There were others downstream.

'All the damn cows are far too close!' Kit said half aloud and Brad heard him, nodding agreement.

'They should be OK, Brad,' Spud Bromley said, an experienced cowhand of many years, pushing forty now. 'Long as the breeze is right an' the powder-smoke don't blow their way. I've seen more stampedes started by a whiff of gunsmoke than a damn Injun raid or a whole bunch of clatterin' noises on a still night.'

Winters was inclined to agree, but he was worried about those cannons: their thunder was a lot heavier than the rattle of six-guns or muskets. 'Wish I'd come alone,' he said wryly. 'You two are cheering me up so much I can't think straight for laughing.'

The cowboys grinned at each other. Then Spud stood in the stirrups, a tall man, thin as a weasel, with eyes like a hawk. 'I think you gonna have to pull rank here, Lieutenant!'

It was mighty infrequent for any of the cowhands to use Brad's old army rank and Winters tensed as he drew up alongside Spud and followed the man's pointing arm.

He could hear the rough laughter and shouting now as he stood in the stirrups and saw a bunch of naked men frolicking in the river, the water clouded from soap and mud stirred up from the bottom. *Damn! Looked like some of them had emptied their bowels at the edge, too!*

On the bank, tilted as if someone had tried to uproot the pole, was a hand-painted sign that had been erected ten days ago. It read:

DRINKING WATER
ONLY HERE
NO WASHING OR SWIMMING
CATTLE GRAZING
DOWNSTREAM

'Soldiers!' gritted Kit Turner. 'Typical!'

Winters urged his mount forward and the others followed down the slope on the river side. One of the skylarking men noticed them, shouted, and wet, rugged faces turned towards the trio as Winters stopped beside the untidy pile of Confederate uniforms on the bank. Brad leaned forward, hands on the saddlehorn.

'You're in Reb country all right, fellers, but the rules still apply. Anyone among you read?'

A bearded man with a broken nose scowled. 'We ain't all ignorant! You Farrell or Winters?'

'Winters.'

'They told us to look out for you. Like to throw your weight around they say.'

'Well, 'they' are wrong. But I do like to have my signs read and obeyed. Cows downstream don't fare too well on soapy water. Or mud — or turds.'

'Aah, it'll be all diluted before it spreads around the bend.' The man struck himself on the wet chest with a big hand. 'I've worked cows before, mister. You're just huntin' trouble, houndin' us this way.'

'You got it wrong, friend. But I do want you out here on the bank — now.'

Brad palmed up his six-gun and heard the rifle levers work behind him as Kit and Spud unsheathed their Winchesters. The swimmers were standing waist deep now, looking to the bearded man for leadership.

'What you gonna do?' the man sneered. 'Put a bullet in us? Or are you usin' blanks already?'

'I was you, mister, I wouldn't want to find out. Just walk out here and get dressed and don't go swimming again and everyone'll be happy.'

'Gee! Ain't he a reg'lar feller?' a

redheaded swimmer said, getting a laugh. 'Treatin' us just like a bunch of naughty l'il schoolboys.'

That brought some yelling, splashing of water, throwing of mud — and open defiance.

Winters just nodded, dismounted, walked over to the pile of clothes and began to toss them up to Kit and Spud who draped them across their saddles. He took some for himself and mounted, watched warily by the now silent men.

'The hell you doin'?' demanded the bearded man.

Winters said nothing, motioned to his men, and they started to ride away, taking the clothes with them. The men shouted and swore, wading ashore. 'Come back here!'

'You had your chance,' Winters called, without turning. He gestured to the four tents that had been pitched back at the brushline. The cowboys rode towards them.

Brad covered the men with his pistol and Spud and Kit roped the tents, pulling them down amidst roaring curses and protests. The swimmers started to surge out of the river, but two shots from Brad's Colt into the gravel stopped them.

'You wanted to stay put, boys — so stay. Kit, drag those tents over to that clear ground and burn 'em. Toss the clothes on when you've got a good fire going.'

Turner hesitated, frowning and Spud pursed his lips but seemed ready to go along with Winters' orders.

'Lend a hand, Spud.'

Turner blew out his cheeks and moved to obey, Spud dismounting. The men tried to make a concerted charge but Winters galloped his mount along the bank only a couple of feet in front of them, spraying them with gravel, forcing them back into the water, clawing at their faces, spitting grit.

By then the first tent was burning.

They stood there, panting, spattered with mud and grit, hair in their faces, wild eyes shifting from the fire to Winters.

'Christ! Have a heart, man! All our stuff's in them tents!' It was the bearded man with the crooked nose pleading.

Winters' battered face didn't change expression, but he called over his shoulder. 'Hold up, Kit. Think these boys've seen the light.' He turned back to the swimmers. '*Have* you, boys?'

They all mumbled in the affirmative, even the bearded loud-mouth.

'OK. Don't burn anything else,' Winters ordered. 'You fellers come on out and sit down there — on the grass if your asses are kinda tender. You read that sign?'

The man hesitated, then nodded. 'Just havin' some fun. Hell, man, it's hot, specially in them uniforms.'

Winters used his gun to point to a low part of the ridge. 'Creek's about twenty yards t'other side — from here, no more'n fifty yards. You can walk that far. And when you get back, you dig a proper latrine, well away from the river. I'll be round to inspect in the morning.'

'What about our clothes?'

'We'll hang 'em on those trees up the slope. Now settle down! We'll pick low branches — this time.'

He raked his hard glare around the group and the bearded man knew what Winters was waiting for. He growled,

'There won't be a next time, but I'll remember you, Winters.'

'Forget me. Just take notice of my signs.'

'You at the original Hashknife Ridge battle?'

'No.'

'Hope you're in this one.'

Winters smiled bleakly. 'If I am, we'll both be on the same side.'

'Now that's somethin' I wouldn't bet on, mister. You are the enemy whatever uniform you wear!'

As they rode away from the sullen 'soldiers', Spud tugged at his axeblade nose and said quietly, 'You seem to be makin' more enemies with your own side than you are with the damn Yankees, Brad.'

Winters smiled thinly. 'Let's go see. They're s'posed to be camped the other side of the ford.'

Both Spud Bromley and Kit Turner looked apprehensive as they touched their spurs to their mounts and rode after the ramrod.

6

The Colonel

The trio were surprised when the Yankees gave them no trouble at all.

Their camp was set up with military precision, twin rows of staggered tents so that in any alarm rushing men would not collide with those coming out of the tent opposite.

Big Joe Briscoe was there, wearing his Union trousers with suspenders over his grubby undershirt, the sleeves pushed up his muscular forearms. Most of the scars from his fight with Winters had disappeared, just a bruise or two still smudging his flesh with fading yellow.

'You got any more complaints, don't bring 'em to me, Winters,' he said, standing near the flap of his tent, holding some papers. 'Colonel's in charge here now.'

Brad Winters stiffened in the saddle. 'Endicott?'

'Colonel Kelvin Endicott, yessir.' Briscoe's hard eyes held the ramrod's gaze steadily. 'B'lieve he's kinda lookin' forward to meetin' you.'

'Likewise.' Brad's voice was thick and he cleared his throat. 'He about?'

Briscoe, half-smiling, jerked his head up the line of tents to one set a little aside from the others. It was larger, too, and there was a collapsible wooden table set up outside with a canvas chair.

'Likely busy. You really gonna bitch about our setup now?'

Winters looked again at the neat rows of tents, the stacked firearms, the mobile kitchen, chimney already smoking, men in Union blue moving about their chores, making the campsite neat and accessible.

'Looks good to me — and you're camped in the area set aside for you. I'll just say howdy to the colonel. Unless you've some objection.'

Briscoe grinned, showing his broken teeth. 'Me? Nah, the colonel can handle a whole passel of curly-wolves like you, Winters.'

'You had a little trouble doin' it,' Kit Turner pointed out and Briscoe chuckled, rubbing his jaw gently.

'I did. But I needed the exercise. You fight pretty damn good for a Reb, Winters.'

'Well, I guess I've fought Yankees who don't hit as hard as you, too. You want to shake on it?'

He leaned from the saddle, right hand outstretched. Briscoe pursed his lips, then shook his head slowly. 'Reckon I'll just let it go. Look for you in the battle, though.'

Winters wondered just what that meant.

'Gonna check-in with this colonel?' asked Kit Turner, a little tensely.

Winters hesitated briefly, then nodded, lifting his reins. 'Let's get it done.' He sounded mighty tense.

A sergeant stepped into their path as

they approached the colonel's tent, holding up a hand.

'Where you bound, Reb?'

Brad nodded towards the tent. 'To see the colonel — I'm Winters.'

The sergeant, a hard-faced man almost as broad as he was tall, spat some tobacco juice as he nodded. 'Figured as much.' He turned and called over his shoulder. 'That reb spoil-sport, Winters, is here, Colonel. You in or out?'

A voice answered from inside the tent. 'Let him wait while I finish this, then send him in.'

Winters was surprised: the voice sounded even enough, but younger than he expected. He dismounted, Kit and Spud staying put. He wasn't expecting it, but in about two minutes he was invited to enter. He ducked into the tent, seeing a shadowy figure bending over a portable writing case on his lap. The man looked up and Brad Winters stopped dead in his tracks.

He was younger than Winters! No

more than his early twenties! *The Endicott he wanted to meet ought to be pushing fifty at least!*

'Come on in, Winters. I believe we need to talk.'

Brad stepped closer, thinking maybe the dim light was playing tricks but, no, this was no middle-aged old soldier. This was a ramrod-straight young officer, clean-shaven, light hair neatly trimmed, a square jaw and eyes that looked as if they could be cold or warm, depending on the situation. Right now they were somewhere in between as they raked the ramrod from hat to boots.

'So, you're the man who killed my father.'

So that was the answer: *son of the original Kel Endicott*, but somehow it still hit him solidly.

'There was a war on, colonel. Your father tortured and murdered my kid brother.'

The eyes were definitely steely now. 'So you say. You'll never know how many times I wished it had been you, not your kin! Did you know he was on that train you blew up?'

'Sure. It was a Confederate hospital train your old man had captured. He killed everyone on board, then loaded it with Yankee ammo and arms. My brother found out and — '

'Enough!' snapped the colonel and the sergeant outside whipped open the tent flap, hand on his gun butt. But Endicott waved him away. He drew down a deep breath and let it out slowly. 'As you say, it was war. For a long time I searched for you, Winters, didn't even know your name at first. I was only a kid, but I wanted to kill the man who had killed my father.'

Winters tensed but said calmly, 'Here I am, Colonel. Your move.'

The younger man frowned. 'You're a hard nut, I see. I did some growing-up when my mother sent me to West Point. You will have gathered that I worshipped my father and wanted to follow in his footsteps. The Point taught me about war and attitudes and I gradually came to terms with my father's death: it was a soldier's death, in action, doing his duty. What more can a warrior ask for?'

Brad nodded slowly, warily. *This Endicott sounded like some kind of fanatic. Well, the Point was noted for 'em.*

'Your brother had vital information — *vital* information. It was imperative that my father knew if he had alerted the enemy before he proceeded with his venture.'

Winters held up a hand. 'All right. It was a long time ago. I've never forgotten Ryan, my brother, or how he looked after your father's interrogation. I settled for the death of your father on that train: kinda poetic justice. It was Joe Briscoe who stirred things up again by letting me think you were the original Colonel Endicott.'

'Well, Joe has a kind of strange sense of humour — and you'd just beaten him in a fight, remember. You can hardly blame him for seizing on some way to salvage at least part of his damaged pride.'

Brad Winters smiled thinly. 'That may be something I'll look into later.' He stood swiftly as he saw the man's face tighten. 'I'm willing to leave it at that, but if you feel you've got to pick up the threads . . . '

The colonel's hatred for Winters was a palpable thing in the tent, but Endicott somehow controlled himself. 'I learned a good deal about you over the years, Winters. I had good contacts I could use at the Point. I wasn't sure what I would do with the knowledge, never, of course, foresaw this opportunity of meeting you face to face.'

He paused and Winters waited silently, alert for trouble, flicking his eyes towards the tent flap and saw the sergeant's shadow on the canvas, staying close.

'I think, for now, I'll leave it lie. You can wonder just what might happen to you during the staging of the battle — I don't believe you deserve any better than that.'

'Colonel, we're supposed to be just *restaging* the battle. Hard to kill a man with blanks.'

'Shooting blanks doesn't guarantee anyone's safety.' Endicott's eyes were cold, his hands clenched.

Winters nodded slightly. 'See you somewhere in the gunsmoke, then, Colonel.'

'I'll be looking for you. Or someone will.'

Endicott remained seated as Winters left, stared at the empty tent entrance for a long time, frowning. He was suddenly aware that he was in the grip of intense emotion: heart thumping against his chest, hands shaking, breathing coming hard, sweat running down his face.

A disturbing meeting . . . with a tough, disturbing man! But the matter must be resolved!

★ ★ ★

105

Reed Galvin was sweating, too — and it wasn't just the close, smoke-thick atmosphere of the back room of Trimble's saloon that caused it: *He was being fleeced!*

He knew now he had made a bad judgment, thinking these visiting businessmen from Denver and Santa Fe were going to be pushovers. They acted kind of stupid, old school pals and, later, in the Confederate Army together. They had taken on a lot of rotgut liquor, sampled the delights offered by Trimble's bar girls and were looking for some new excitement with the cards. *They said*.

They joked with each other about the girls and the various positions they claimed to have enjoyed — one man even brought up some old school stories about their first tentative and clumsy encounters with the opposite sex. It started a seemingly endless round of anecdotes and Galvin was hard put to keep their — and his own — concentration on the cards. When it was their turn to deal, they did so in what seemed an indifferent and automatic manner, the pasteboards skimming in blurs at *professional* speed. *Damn!* Why hadn't he been alert enough to note that kind of thing?

He had been too slow realizing that he had been losing steadily, and that they had been deliberately distracting him. *Outsmarted at his own game!*

His brain was clouded with whiskey fumes. He now believed they'd managed to put something in his drink. He was losing so consistently that he began to suspect they had come in with the express purpose of fleecing him: put on their half-drunk act with all its interruptions so as to make *his* concentration sloppy. *And they'd damn well succeeded!*

The ginger-headed one with the almost orange-coloured beard and moustache, suddenly said in a voice that sounded like a saw cutting through steel, 'I b'lieve that card you just dealt yourself don't count, mister, seein' as it came off the bottom of the deck!'

Conversation was dead and buried on the instant and a tense stillness suddenly filled that corner of the room. All eyes were on Reed Galvin and the sweat popped out of his glands. One raking glance told him he was right: he *had* been set up! Falling for their act, losing his focus, allowing them to fleece him without realizing it. Now they were wrapping it all up by accusing him of cheating. It had the smell of — revenge, somehow. *Well, he had done a little bottom-dealing up-river a few weeks ago. Could he have stepped on their toes without knowing it?*

'You'd need an army telescope to see through this smoke screen,' he answered slowly. 'And you *still* couldn't've seen any bottom-deck dealin' — *because it never happened!*'

He was shouting and thrusting to his feet now as chairs clattered over backward and the four players jumped up together, all reaching for their guns. Reed Galvin's Sheriff's Special came smoothly into his hand and three fast shots roared, the concussion making the overhead lamp sway jerkily, throwing moving shadows over the tumbling bodies. Two went down, hard and clattering. A third tried to reach the door, tripped over a chair and rammed his head into the wall. He fell, dazed and bleeding. The fourth man had his gun half-drawn, suddenly thrust his hands so high and fast and with such effort that he brought himself up on his toes.

'Don't shoot!' he bleated, as the door opened and Mr Meeker came in with a gun in his gloved hand, crouching, cold, black eyes taking in the scene.

'Who sent you?' demanded Galvin, trying to keep the tremor out of his voice. He jerked his gun and the man winced.

'Rancher in Walsenberg — said you clipped his son.'

Reed Galvin kept his face blank. He knew who the man meant and he had cleaned-out a drunken young cowboy so as to get a stake to come here.

Trimble himself appeared suddenly and, behind him, men who had left their drinks or painted women to come see what all the shooting was about. The saloon man came in, kicking the door half-closed on the gawkers. Mr Meeker still kept his gun cocked.

'And what in the name of Jesus have we got here, Galvin?' Trimble's fleshy face was beet red.

Reed felt better now he had figured what had happened. He could fast talk his way out of this, no trouble. Still with his smoking gun in his hand, his voice was strong and steady as he explained succinctly.

'They set me up! Sonuvers come here acting drunk, telling stupid jokes, playing recklessly, let me win a hand or two, and I fell for it. Suddenly, I'm almost broke and the bastards were getting ready to take my last coupla dollars by accusing me of card-sharping.'

'Your fault, the whole blamed thing,' Trimble cut in harshly and Mr Meeker stepped up alongside his boss. 'You're responsible for choosin' the men you play with. If they were card-sharps and you didn't pick 'em, then don't come bitchin' to me.'

Reed's eyes narrowed. 'I'm not bitching. I'm telling you what happened. They cold-decked me and were about to shoot me full of holes, but I was faster.'

'Tell it to the sheriff,' Trimble said coldly, opening the door and calling to the curious crowd, 'Someone go fetch Slade Samson.' Then he nodded to Meeker who stepped forward, holding out his gloved left hand towards Galvin, his gun covering the gambler. 'I'll take your gun.'

Reed hesitated but one look into those dark, pitiless eyes and he let the gun swivel on its trigger guard and handed it to Mr Meeker. Galvin swung his gaze to Trimble.

'Reckon I can get my money back off these damn sharpies?' Reed gestured to the dead men.

'You leave 'em set till Slade gets here. Whatever they got on 'em belongs to the house, anyway. You better hope this one still standin' and t'other that's hit his head backs your story. Slade might just run you outa town . . . and think yourself damn lucky if that's all he does.'

'Goddamn! I protected myself! It wasn't my doing!'

'No one else's,' the saloon man pointed out. 'You're finished here. And there's no return on your bond, either.'

Galvin felt the sweat ooze from him again. This time it was icy cold. 'Great to see how you stand by your house-men, Trimble!'

The saloon man didn't even flinch. 'I make the rules. You best sit down, Galvin. You don't look too spry.'

No damn wonder! Here he was, broke, fired, facing possible time in jail, or maybe a gun-whipping from Meeker. Hell, he didn't even have a horse.

He sighed and dropped disconsolately into his chair.

Whatever had made him think his luck was going to change for the better by coming to this lousy town! He was not only worse off than when he arrived, he was worse off than he had ever been for the last twenty years.

The sheriff, when he came, listened to his story in silence. The two, shaky surviving gamblers, fast sobering now, reluctantly backed him up, looking warily at Meeker.

The man who had struck his head on the wall said, 'He'd fleeced the son of a friend of ours in Walsenburg. We were just squarin' things.'

'I ask you if that's true, I guess you'll deny it,' Slade Samson said to Galvin who nodded vigorously.

''Course I will! I don't deal from the bottom or mark my cards.'

Samson grunted. 'Might shake your hand after, Galvin. You'd be the first travellin' gambler I ever met who don't mark his cards or hide an ace up his sleeve.'

Reed Galvin licked his lips. 'Point is,

Sheriff, they fleeced me and then tried to shoot me.' He looked around at the crowd at the now open door. 'Someone must've seen or heard somethin'?

A couple of men confirmed that Reed had only been defending himself, but thought that he *might* have been playing with a stacked deck.

They tossed it back and forth and, in the end, Samson bellowed for silence, holding fingertips to his temples.

'Enough, for Chris'sake! I already got a headache like I been hit with a sledgehammer. My jail's full to over-flowin' and a prisoner with a minor head wound somehow died in his cell an' that ain't been satisfactorily explained.' He turned bleak eyes to Galvin. 'I know you ain't as innocent as you claim. I got no papers on you, but I don't aim to knowingly leave a card-slick in place to cause more trouble later on.'

'Sheriff, I swear I never dealt no bottom cards!' Galvin's sweating was worse than ever now. 'I was just — '

'You was just leavin', that's what

you're doin',' Slade Samson said flatly. He flicked his gaze to Trimble. 'I know you likely got a raw deal from Trimble there. He's a miserable cuss, but that makes no nevermind. I got enough troubles without takin' yours on, too.' He jerked his head towards the door. 'Light a shuck, Galvin. You be gone in an hour, or I'll toss you in my cells, even if I have to use a shoehorn to fit you in.'

Reed Galvin shot a poisonous look at Trimble and Mr Meeker, and pushed his way out. He wiped some of the sweat off his face: no use pushing his luck.

But he would have to ride the rails out of town. He didn't have enough to even buy a ticket on the next train out. He would have to get himself stowed aboard somehow, and stay hidden until it left the siding.

'Hey, hold up a minute, gambler!' a deep voice called.

On his way to the railroad depot, Galvin turned slowly, right hand creeping under his jacket. Two men were coming towards him, hardcases he had seen in the saloon; might have even sat in on a hand or two. He smiled crookedly.

'Too late if you want my wallet, gents. Nothing in it.'

'Relax,' Mort Tibbetts said, forcing an unaccustomed smile, but Griffin kept his face deadpan as he came up beside him. 'You had some bad luck, but you did pretty good with that hideaway gun. You got a minute, mebbe we can tell you how you can put somethin' worthwhile in that empty wallet. You game?'

Reed Galvin knew they were likely thieves or cutthroats of some kind; no mistaking that look. But he was desperate right now, and he thought he could outsmart these two, if he had to. So, he said, 'I got an hour before I have to leave.'

'Plenty of time then,' Tibbetts told him confidently. 'Come on over to that doorway. We got us a bottle to help make things a little more pleasant. You're smart, we can make all your dreams come true.'

7

Troubles

Brad Winters was slowly getting mad — at Matt Farrell.

The man was so involved in this damn Battle Day — now the official name of the staging of the Hashknife Ridge action — that he was hardly ever at the Block F. He spent most of his time in town meeting with the newly formed Battle Day Committee. The ramrod was tired of sending men into town with messages for Farrell, or, worse having to go himself when an important decision was required.

He had enough problems just running the spread as it was, and time was short and getting shorter. The cowboys tended to leave their chores or do them quickly and unsatisfactorily just so they could slip up to the Ridge and have a look at the growing encampment there. And it wasn't the precise lines of Confederate or Union tents or the men playing at 'soldiers' that attracted them: there was a fast-growing encampment of spectators setting up out there now as almost all accommodation in the town was booked. And there were 'ladies' at the campsite who sought to make themselves an income while they waited for the big day to arrive. They organized into a group, calling themselves The Pussycats, and hired bodyguards.

Their prices undercut those of the whores who worked The Comet in town and trouble was a'brewing. It had already erupted on a couple of occasions as bouncers from The Comet came out to the camp where the newcomers were plying their rival trade and confronted the men who protected the interlopers.

There had been two vicious brawls and one of the 'protectors', while in town having a few relaxing drinks, afterwards was found in a back alley that ran down to the creek, beaten and kicked half to death. He was lying on his side with his bleeding face in the murky water when found by Boney Carson and some of the boys he ran with, including the frightening Frog Delaney. Frog, ever practical, started going through the man's pockets but Boney, wanting to stay in Sheriff Samson's good books, ran and told the lawman about the man.

It was clear his injuries were a rough warning from the bouncers of The Comet. But Slade Samson, a good lawman, mostly, knew damn well he wasn't going to get anywhere with an investigation into this. The best he could do was issue his own warnings. The Comet owners and staff, while denying any knowledge of how the half-drowned man had received his injuries, agreed they would stay clear of trouble: the sheriff surely must know how well-behaved they were — *sure, sure!*

Sheriff Samson rode out to the

encampment of The Pussycats, the name now written in tar on a splintered plank fixed to a nearby tree, and was given an assurance that *they* would keep a low profile and avoid trouble like the bubonic plague. He sighed and knew the easy given promises were the best he could hope for. But when he was mounting his weary horse, one of the women, young and carrot-haired, sidled up and offered him 'comfort' if he wished it. 'Kinda goodwill gesture,' she told him seductively, letting him see her cleavage as she moved around him languorously. 'All free . . . an' maybe you could let it be known around town just how good The Pussycats are . . .'

'Lady, the only thing I'm mountin' is my hoss here,' he said, grunting as he settled into leather. He touched a hand to his hatbrim. 'But obliged for the offer.'

'Any time, Sheriff — just ask for Flame.'

He rode out quickly, stopped at the Block F ranch house but neither Matt

Farrell nor Brad Winters was there.

'Dunno where Matt is,' Spud Bromley told him, 'but Brad's somewhere out on the range — camps out a lot these days, tryin' to control them fools at the Ridge, keep 'em where they're s'posed to be, an' not traipsin' all over our range.'

'You tell Brad there's trouble a'brewin' out there. A rival bunch of whores has set 'emselves up and one of their bodyguards has already been beat half to death. Tell Brad I want him to keep an eye on 'em. I can't be in two places at once.'

Later, when the message was delivered, Spud took a step back as he saw the change in the ramrod's face. It was already glistening with sweat and smeared with dirt, and had a new cut on the jawline from a flailing hoof during branding work he was engaged in. Now it turned decidedly ugly and Winters flung down the hot branding iron.

'God *damn* Slade Samson! I ain't

121

doing his job for him — I got enough on, trying to keep this ranch going as it is.'

Spud nodded sympathetically, scratched at his stubbled jaw. 'Yeah, I guess you're right, Brad. But I don't like the sounds of a feud startin' up with them Pussy-cats and The Comet whores. Could get mighty nasty.'

'And all on our range!' Winters let loose a stream of curses and slowly they drifted away into the sunshine. He pulled off his stained and torn work-gloves, dropped them beside the glowing coals of the branding fire. 'Spud, take over here, and tell Kit to start bringing up the horses and get 'em stowed in the outer canyons. I'm riding into town to have it out with Matt.'

'Aw — mebbe I better come along . . .?'

'Mebbe you better do like I said.' Brad Winters was in no mood for arguing and Bromley quickly recognized it. The other men in the branding crew did, too; kept silent as the ramrod took a drink from the big work canteen hanging from a tree branch, poured water over his sweating head and then went to his patient horse.

Settling in saddle he raked the watching cowboys with a hard glare. 'What the hell're you standing around for? There's a whole slew of them mavericks in that there pen — and they better all be carrying the Block F brand when I get back!'

He wrenched his mount's head around and spurred away. Monkey Tarr whistled softly. 'Ain't seen Brad that mad in a coon's age.'

'You'll see him a lot madder, he comes back an' finds we ain't finished the brandin',' growled Bromley, waving the smoking iron. 'C'mon, let's get to it!'

★ ★ ★

What made Winters madder than usual was the way Samson had gone about this. The sheriff was leery of Matt Farrell — Brad suspected Matt's wealth kind of intimidated the lawman — so instead of telling Farrell to have someone keep an eye on brewing trouble at the Ridge, he told Brad and left it to him to sort things out with the Block F rancher.

Well, Brad Winters aimed to do just that — and this afternoon, by hell! He had had enough. The town was ecstatic with the way the money was rolling in from the visitors who were still flocking here by wagons, special stage runs, by horseback, train and even by walking. He figured if they could work out some way to fly they would damned well do that, too. The crush of people, horses and street traffic did nothing to improve his mood.

He didn't know just where Matt was in town but knew he had some arrangements to make about the safe stowing of the Civil War firearms. Always efficient, Matt had insured everything, even against heavy rain washing out the Battle Day, and now had to make certain all details complied

with the insurance company's require-
ments.

'Just in case anything does go wrong,
and I have to make a claim,' he had
explained to Brad, one night after
supper, but the ramrod had merely
grunted: he had little interest in the
whole blamed shebang. Just wanted it
over and done with.

So he stabled his horse at the livery
and asked the hostler, Dub McLean, if
he had seen Matt.

'Seen him earlier down by the crick,
just past the end of our holdin' pens.
He — ' Dub broke off and while
Winters waited, the man shrugged,
picked up a fork and began turning
over the hay pile. 'Aw, don't matter.
They're gone by now, anyway.'

'Who's gone, Dub?' Winters grabbed
his arm.

Dub sniffed, leaned on his long
fork handle. 'Well, it's them hardcases
— the one you got into a fight with in
the saloon, an' the feller he hangs with
— Tibbetts.'

'I know who you mean.' Brad recalled the one called Tibbetts giving him some kind of veiled warning because he had 'put two of his friends out of action': he still didn't know why the man had said it.

'Matt was talkin' with 'em. Not sure it was all friendly. I-I didn't want to butt in. They all looked kinda mean, though, Matt, too.'

Winters was only half-listening now: *what was Matt doing talking with two hardcases like that, and in such an out of the way place?*

'That feller you winged when he nearly shot the sheriff,' Dub said suddenly, his words penetrating Brad's thoughts, 'he died in jail, you know.'

'What? It was only a scalp wound. Doc said it wasn't serious.'

'There was that big brawl with The Comet bouncers and them Pussycats' bodyguards. Samson threw everyone in sight into jail, includin' that feller Griffin: he was caught up in the fight, several townsmen and visitors, too.

Anyways, the cells've been bustin' at the seams for days and when Ty Carver opened up for breakfast, he found this feller McVeeters dead, jammed under a bunk. They figure he tried to get outa the crush but the bunk collapsed with so many others on it an' he suffocated. No one knew he was under there.'

Winters nodded. 'OK, long as I'm not being blamed.' He flipped the hostler a coin before he turned and walked away. 'Obliged, Dub.'

He found Matt Farrell in the private room the town council used for their meetings, in the back of the saloon; a lot of such meetings were very dry affairs and the room was handy for refreshments to help things go more amicably. There were three men with Matt: Bede Halstrom, Captain Johnson from the fort and Tom O'Neil, the gunsmith. Brad excused himself and asked to see Matt right away.

'Can't it wait a few minutes, Brad? We're about through here and — '

'We are through here, Matt,' said the Captain, rising and reaching for his hat. 'I've a regimental inspection, anyway, so I have to be going. Bede and Tom don't have any more queries . . . ? No. You've handled things with your usual competence, Matt.'

The storekeeper and gunsmith said they were satisfied with the meeting and the trio left. Matt frowned, not pleased.

'Well, what the hell's so important you couldn't make a decision for yourself, Brad? Damnit, I pay you ramrod's wages to — '

'You won't be paying me much longer, this damn Battle Day keeps interrupting my work,' Brad Winters cut in sharply and Matt stopped, saw the man was really angry and knew better than to try to throw his weight around unnecessarily.

He lifted his hands, patting the air. 'Take it easy, Brad — what's happened now?'

'It's what's gonna happen.' Winters told him about the sheriff's visit and the looming trouble between the ladies of the night from The Comet and The Pussycats. 'Gonna be a brawl bigger than the Battle of Hashknife Ridge and I want no part of it.'

Matt swore softly. 'We don't need that kind of thing. Damnit, Slade's not doing his job properly, expecting us to keep an eye on 'em — just because it's all on my land, I guess. I'll have a word with him.'

Winters locked his gaze steadily in Matt's face and said quietly, 'Hear you been having a word with them hardcases, Tibbetts, and that bull, Griffin, too.'

Farrell stiffened. 'What gave you the idea I even know — what's his name? Tibbetts?'

'Someone said you were talking to him and Griffin down by the creek behind the livery.'

'Oh, those two.' Matt shook his head briefly. 'Braced me about that shooting when you saved Samson's neck and your fight with Griffin later. Said I'd better keep a tight rein on you, or you'd be in a heap of trouble.'

Winters let it sink in, then nodded slowly. 'There's something funny about that. He warned me off after the fight with Griffin, too — think I told you.'

'You did. I told him he had any beef to take it up with you, not me.'

Winters smiled crookedly. 'Well, that's telling 'em, all right, Matt. That's really telling 'em.'

Farrell started to frown then smiled and punched Brad lightly on the shoulder. 'Ah, hell, I was mad at them stopping me that way. Too damn busy for that kinda piss-ant thing — I'll mention it when I see the sheriff.'

'Forget it — I'm not worried about Tibbetts. You got time for a drink?'

Matt Farrell pulled out his gold pocket watch, flipped open the lid and shook his head. 'Not if I have to go see Slade now. I'm due at the bank to check with Ethan Handy about his arrangements for keeping all that money. His safe must be busting at the seams by now. You go have a few beers.

'Fact, why not stay overnight? You've earned a break.'

'Might just do that, Matt. Been feeling a mite edgy.'

'Fine. Use my hotel room. I'll drift on back to the spread after I see Handy.' He gave one of his charming smiles. 'Guess I've kind of been neglecting it lately.'

'You have,' Winters agreed bluntly.

Matt grinned and hurried out. Winters rolled and lit a cigarette before leaving. *Yeah, he liked the idea of a night in town now. He had been over-working. Best to take a break before he broke . . .*

★ ★ ★

But he wondered about the wisdom of his decision a few hours later when, sleeping in Matt Farrell's mighty comfortable feather bed, specially imported for him by the hotel, he was wakened by breaking glass — followed swiftly by the blast of the twin barrels of a shotgun.

At the first crack and tinkle of the glass Brad rolled out of the bed, on the side furthest away from the window, an instant before the shot-gun thundered and the expensive mattress was reduced to a snow-storm of singed and torn feathers and smouldering calico.

He snatched his six-gun from the chair beside the bed, slithered under the frame and saw the outline of the killer through the shattered window, frantically trying to reload his smoking weapon.

Winters came out with a rush, lifting to his knees, fanning the gun hammer. Glass shards flew and the timber frame splintered — and the outline of the killer disappeared. Ears still ringing with the explosions, Brad still distinctly heard the balcony rail give way, a brief, startled cry and then a commotion in the street below.

There was also a commotion at the hotel-room door, frantic fists hammering on the heavy panels, a shaky voice demanding to know what was going on in there.

Holding the smoking Colt down at his side, Brad walked across and unlocked the door.

So much for a restful night's sleep.

8

Tension

''Course, he mightn't've been after you at all, Brad,' Sheriff Slade Samson said. He was seated in his office, looking drawn and very tired. He stifled a yawn. 'I mean, you were usin' Matt Farrell's room, sleepin' in Matt's bed . . . '

Winters, feeling edgy and tired after the shotgun incident nodded briefly. 'Thought of that. This Tibbetts *hombre* and his pard, Griffin, told Matt to warn me off. They were riled over me shooting McVeeters and brawling with Griffin.'

'I got two deputies scourin' the town for 'em, but the one you shot off the balcony never lived long enough to say anythin' useful. He's not from around here, but I know for a fact he sometimes rides with those renegades we got livin' back in the hills.' He snapped his fingers suddenly. 'Hell, you might know him, come to think of it. He was with Frank Astor's bunch when they tried to rustle some of Block F cattle — musta been, aw . . . how long ago was that? His name was Scully, if memory serves correctly.'

'That was before last winter. I don't think I've ever had a run-in with him. I'd've hanged him if I'd've caught him, but that was a long time ago.'

'Well, you won't be runnin' into him again this side of Hell.' Samson squinted. 'You sure do draw trouble like a magnet, Brad. You gonna be in town long?'

Winters smiled crookedly. 'Heading back to Block F come morning, Slade, rest easy.'

'By God, not till this goddamn Battle Day is over! I could use another six deputies. Ethan Handy tells me there's sixty to eighty thousand in the bank's safe right now. And still growin'! Too damn much responsibility for my likin'.'

'Helluva lot, all right.' Winters was impressed, 'But people are spending big, despite prices going through the roof.'

'Judas, don't talk to me about that! I been getting complaints from locals — they gotta pay the same as the visitors.'

'They're all making something out of the deal no matter who they are. You finished with me, Slade? I need to get some shut-eye.'

'Just sign your statement and we're all through.'

The hotel wouldn't allow him to use the buckshot-riddled room again so he slept in the livery hayloft. Dub woke him early and he was on the trail before full daylight. Despite the attempt on his life, he felt more relaxed and there was noticeable relief on the ranch crew's faces when he appeared at the breakfast-table in the dogrun and handed out his day's orders in a mild, easy manner.

Matt Farrell was shocked and not a

little worried when Brad told him about the shot-gunner.

'Hell, it could've been meant for me! I been coming down a mite hard on some folk, about them raising their prices way too much. I've had some arguments, a couple threats, but I didn't take 'em seriously.' He paused, pursing his lips. 'Think Tibbetts might've hired Scully?'

'I dunno — I'm not gonna let it bother me. I'll be getting out to the range again, Matt. We're driving most of the remuda up to the holding canyons, well away from the battle site. That's if we don't get any interruptions.' Brad looked pointedly at Farrell who smiled slowly and raised his hands out from his sides.

'Promise to leave you be. I gotta go into town again and officially welcome the pipe band arriving on the train, anyway!'

'The what?'

'The St Andrews Pipe and Drum Band. The Scottish Association in

Denver's sending 'em down. Should be a good added attraction, something different. Not many folk here would've seen or heard Scottish bagpipes. Might try to organize a little Highland tournament, too, tossing the caber or sword dancing . . . it'll work out well, I reckon.'

Winters sighed heavily shaking his head. 'You missed your calling, Matt. You should leave running the ranch to me and make a career for yourself arranging medicine shows.'

'Now there's a thought!'

That was enough for Winters. He lost no time in getting back to what he loved best: rough, tough, sweaty, muscle-wrenching ranch work in God's wide open spaces.

A man could see something substantial for his efforts that way — might never be cash-rich but he wouldn't have a bellyful of ulcers spoiling his appetite, either.

★ ★ ★

'By God, we got us a tough one in that damn ramrod Farrell uses.' Griffin made the obvious statement as he ate breakfast noisily and gustily, while Tibbetts poked at his food and looked surly. The man glanced up irritably.

'Whyn't you tell me somethin' I don't know!'

Griffin shrugged, used to Tibbetts's see-sawing moods. 'Should've let me do it instead of hirin' that deadbeat, Scully — Winters'd be dead by now.'

'Or you would be. In any case, you were already in jail waitin' to shut McVeeters' mouth before he started singin' like a canary just to get out: he hated closed-in spaces.'

'Well, he won't know whether his coffin's a tight fit or not.'

'It's too bad, though — Hal was good with safes. Hell, we're losin' men to Winters every time we turn around! Damn the son of a bitch! I ain't gonna let him get away with it. We'll just have to see he's taken care of in the fight. *Some*'ll be usin' live ammo.'

'Christ, they're mad! Big deal like this and they just cain't forget they was licked by the Johnny Rebs fifteen years ago! So they gotta try and square things!' He shook his head. 'They'll never get away with it.'

'Never mind what they might or might not get away with: it's what we can get away with that counts.'

'Well, the gambler seems OK. He's lyin' low, enjoyin' that Flame I hear, from the Pussycats. Chip an' Wiley oughta be showin' any day now.'

'They're damn well late!' Tibbetts gritted, fist slamming down on his thigh, face almost tormented now, the tension building within him. 'Nothin's fallin' into place!'

Griffin paused with a mouthful of coffee, looking at the man over the rim of his tin cup.

'He ain't gonna show his face in town the way Samson's got his deputies runnin' around with a fistful of wanted dodgers, checkin' the pictures against new arrivals, Mort.'

'He should *be* here. *Now!* Judas, it's only a coupla days till they stage the battle. The train's due and I'm worried that damn banker's gonna panic and send the money back to Denver early.'

Griffin nodded. 'Be a helluva thing if that happens.'

'It ain't gonna happen!' Mort Tibbetts snapped, his face suddenly easing of some of the tension. 'There's one way to make sure. I din' wanta tip our hand so soon, but it'll guarantee Mr Ethan Handy keeps his safe stuffed to burstin' with all that cash — until we're good and ready to relieve him of it.'

★ ★ ★

Matt Farrell sat back sharply in his chair in the private room of the hotel restaurant where he was having his supper. Opposite him sat the banker, Ethan Handy, pale and fidgety, flabby face gleaming with sweat. He kept taking his spectacles off and polishing the lenses as if they were constantly steaming up.

'What the hell is the matter with you, Ethan? You look like someone's just given you the death sentence.'

The banker's jowls quivered as he shook his head emphatically. 'No, no, something I had for lunch, I think, didn't agree with me.'

'Something sure didn't. Now why have you interrupted my supper? I thought we'd concluded our business.'

Handy mopped his face once more, leaned his elbows on the table, shoulders hunching a little. 'I-I've had a telegraph from head office in Denver, Matt. They — they don't want me to send the money through on the train.'

Farrell frowned, stared levelly at the banker, but the man wouldn't meet his gaze. The rancher set down his fork and dabbed at his mouth with the edge of his table napkin.

'I thought they were eager for you to get all that cash out of this town and into their hands?'

'So did I! They seemed that way, but now they feel it's too risky. An unescorted train and so on.'

'Well, Captain Johnson can spare a few men as guards, I dare say.'

'No!' The banker almost shouted it, his manner causing Matt's gathering frown to deepen. 'I-I've spoken to him, but he said you wanted all his men committed to the battle show and he had worked so hard at rearranging his schedules and patrol rosters that *nothing* will make him change the arrangements again. He's most emphatic.'

Matt sighed, mouth a thin line now. 'Ethan, this is an added complication I can do without — I've enough things to worry about already. What you're saying in effect is the money stays put — till when? After Battle Day?'

'Yes, yes. After it's over. After the battle, Colonel Endicott and his men'll be returning north on the train — they can form a more-than-adequate guard, so we're to send the money along with them. I'll have to try and arrange it.'

'You got the telegraph with you?' Farrell half-held out a hand but Handy shook his head.

'No, I didn't think it necessary to bring it.'

Matt's teeth tugged at his lower lip, gaze on the uncomfortable banker all the time. He nodded slowly. 'Well, it's up to Denver, I suppose. Don't they realize the danger of leaving so much money here with the town bursting with all kinds of hardcases? Helluva risk, Ethan!'

'Don't I know it! I haven't slept since the crowds started arriving.' He stood abruptly, sounding short of breath. 'All right, Matt. I'm sorry it's complicated things but it's out of my hands. Now I have to be getting back.'

'You've got time for a drink, haven't you? Steady you down — you look as if you can use one.'

'No! No, I'm sorry. Eloise will have supper waiting.'

The man practically ran from the room and Farrell frowned. There was something odd about this whole damn thing!

He gulped down his coffee, threw his napkin onto the table then hurried out himself. There was one thing he could do to help clear up the mystery anyway . . . or partly so.

Fifteen minutes later, Farrell was frowning when he stepped out of the telegraph office, tagged on to one end of the railroad depot.

He paused to light a cheroot, shook out the match and then continued to frown as he walked back towards town. Halfway there he stopped, hand dropping to his gun butt: two figures were running between the buildings on the edge of town and the way they were moving it was clear one was the fugitive, the other the pursuer.

Even as he watched the second gained on the first and brought him down with a flying tackle. Matt still stood, one hand on his Colt butt, cheroot in the other. The second man straddled the tackled one and his arms flailed as he began beating his captive who let out a howl that sounded more like a woman.

Matt sprinted forward. The attacker was swinging his arms at Gatling-gun speed as he punched the pinned victim.

'Stop! Stop it, Frog! I never told, I swear — Owwww!' Blood spurted from a mashed nose and lips.

Farrell recognized them as two of the town's young hooligans, Frog Delaney and the skinny, near half-witted one they called Boney. They were always in some kind of a scrape. Matt grabbed Frog's upraised fist, brought a yell from the youth as he dragged him off Boney.

'Lemme go! Lemme go! I just found out he told the sheriff it was me put the salts in the hoss trough on Dowd.'

'I never meant to, Mr Farrell!' denied Boney, behind the rancher now, wiping his bloody face. 'It just slipped out!'

'Liar! I'm gonna beat your goddamn head in!'

Matt was having trouble holding the struggling Frog and gestured to Boney.

'Go on — clear off while you can.'

Boney ran away fast, deeper into the town, weaving down the alleys and side streets he knew so well. Frog slowly stopped struggling, turned his sweating, ratlike face to look at Matt.

'My old man'll knock you into the middle of next week, you lay a hand on me again!'

'I'm shaking in my shoes, Frog.' Farrell pushed him away so roughly the youth fell to hands and knees. 'Go on, get away from me. Light a shuck before I kick your butt.'

'I'm goin', but don't think you'll get away with it . . . ' Frog sniffed hard, spitting towards the rancher.

Matt took a threatening step forward and grinned to himself as Frog took off like a scared fawn.

'Damn' fool kids,' he said, and kept on his own path towards the bank building. He saw the residential section was already in darkness. He swore softly, hesitated: should he knock on the door anyway or — ? *No, leave it for tonight.*

He decided to call on Handy tomorrow — and see what kind of a story he came up with to explain how come there hadn't been a telegraph message for him from Denver for nigh on a week.

It ought to make mighty interesting listening.

9

Preliminaries

The spectators' campsites had been kept part way up the slopes, towards the narrow top of the ridge, away from the bivouacs and tent-lines of the opposing 'armies'. There were dozens, scores, even hundreds of tents — and other sites were merely open spaces with bedrolls spread on the ground. The nights were becoming a little chill but no one seemed to mind, built fires in rock circles and huddled close. Someone said the camp was on the 'knife-edge' of Hashknife Ridge and that became the name from then on: Camp Knife Edge.

Excitement was building as Battle Day fast approached. There had been a few brawls between the Yankees and the Rebs but, so far, nothing too serious in the way of injuries. Bede Halstrom's wagons brought in loads of food and supplies such as had been available on the battlefields of fifteen years ago. It gave an added dimension to the enjoyment of the eager spectators to be able to say they were eating the same kind of food 'their boys' had consumed back in 1864. There were even authentic ex-army cooks on hand to demonstrate how the food had been prepared, although the cooking facilities at the camp were slightly better and more convenient than the Confederate and Union armies had enjoyed all those years ago. At least here they could light their cooking fires and move about the camp without worrying about enemy snipers trying to pick them off.

The stews were little different to what was served up in frontier homes every day, and many of the spectators added their own herbs and spices, anyway, few of which would have been available to soldiers under war conditions. They baked their Johnny-cake bread but the womenfolk added yeast so that what they ate was very little different to what would be on their supper tables any day of the week — bearing no resemblance to the iron-hard mud-cakes that the army had had to endure, some so hard they could only be broken with a rifle butt. No one liked the boiled jerky, served up by the cooks in deference to civilian teeth and jaws unused to chomping leatherhard strips. They complained to Captain Johnson.

'Repugnant as it may be, folks, I'm afraid it's the kind of grub they serve us up. We want you to enjoy your experience so we'll knock some of the rough edges off here and there, use a mite more flavouring and spices. I'm sure you'll find that much more to your liking.'

The captain hurriedly sent one of his privates to find some committee member who could better handle the situation . . .

The uniforms were authentic, obtained from old army stores in St Louis and a museum in Atlanta that had its stockrooms overflowing with unused army-issue items, from boots to can-teens, belts and beyond. Bede Halstrom had some spares — North and South — in his store in case they were needed.

Matt Farrell had enlisted some of the current army officers and men from the fort to introduce regulation camp routine and parades for the entertainment of the spectators. Captain Johnson complained bitterly that there had been none of that at the original battle of Hashknife Ridge.

'Good God, Matt! There was no time for that sort of thing! It was almost totally disorganized — we were a rabble, on the run, trapped ourselves down here below the ridge, and when the Yankees came after us we fought like hell because we knew we had to or be slaughtered. There was none of this parading, or queueing for meals, sure not saluting — everything went by the board until the fighting started and then army training took over because they knew if they didn't fight as they'd been trained to, they were dead men.'

Matt Farrell kept nodding as the red-faced captain spoke, took his arm. 'Yes, Captain, I understand, but these folk have paid good money to see an army *show*. They expect something besides the actual re-enactment of the battle. The history books report this as one of the most desperate and hard-fought last stands of the Confederate Army which turned into a glorious victory. It had no effect on the war's outcome, but folk have their own pictures of what went on in their heads. We have to give them *something* of their vision and not all the blood-and-guts and suffering that really took place. Let 'em see men salute an officer, stand at attention on parade, go through their drill routine, blow a few bugles. Why, they'll be telling their grandchildren about this. We're obligated to entertain them, Captain. Obligated!'

'You wanted authenticity you said. At every meeting of the committee you emphasized *authenticity* damnit!'

'Yes, yes, in the battle itself! That *has* to pretty well match what's in the history books, but in the preliminaries like this, we can make it more relaxed — the people will feel more involved and — '

Then the captain jumped as there was a strange sound coming up the draw. He looked wildly at Matt. 'My God! What's that?'

Farrell smiled. '*That* is the skirl o' the pipes, laddie — the St Andrews Scottish Pipe and Drum band.'

'Oh, sweet Jesus! Men in skirts, strangling some sort of instrument, or unfortunate animal under their arms! This is too much, Matt! You're going to start a riot, man — no Civil War battle that I know of was ever like this!'

'It's *entertainment*, Cap'n. That's the name of the game. Give the people their money's worth, something to talk about, spread the word. Next year will be even bigger.'

Johnson glared at Matt as people stopped in their tracks and stared at the approaching Scots, the drum major with his tall bearskin busby out front tossing and juggling his silver-headed staff in a truly adroit and dexterous manner.

'Matt, you should be selling snake-oil!' the captain said in disgust and stormed away.

Farrell looked with pride on his surprise innovation, gazed around, saw the awe and astonishment, the dumb-founded expressions of the crowd — and the excitement of the kids and younger adults at this presentation of something most had not even heard of, let alone seen. Some cheered the drum major after an intricate contortion to catch his twirling, descending staff from a truly awesome height.

Then a deep, mocking voice bel-lowed, above the growing sounds of the cheering, 'Hey, ladies, someone's cut your dresses too short! The sight of all them knobbly knees is al-mighty dis-gustin'! Oooooo — I'm plumb offended!'

Silence except for the skirl of the pipes — suddenly dwindling as the words drifted down into the draw. The drum major, clutching his staff with white knuckled hands, turned quickly to the slowing pipers and drummers.

'Now, lads! Ignore this! We should be used to such insults from ignorant colonials . . . '

The Scottish brogue was heavy and most of his words were unintelligible to the crowd, but the word 'ignorant' was clear enough and suddenly men were running down the slopes, incensed, as the bandsmen hurriedly stacked their pipes and drums and turned to meet the charge.

Matt Farrell stood rooted to the spot and then abruptly began to move, trying to interject himself between the two factions before they met. This was one Battle of Hashknife Ridge he hadn't anticipated.

It would probably be remembered long after the events of the re-enactment of the real battle had faded from memory. These mostly sallow-faced young foreigners in their resplendent kilts and jewel-hilted *skean-dhu* short knives tucked into the rolled tops of their knee-length socks, cocked their fists, eager to meet the roaring, charging roughnecks tearing towards them.

They clashed with flying fists and feet and one red-haired Scot with a face like old oak bark, effortlessly lifted man after man over his head and threw them like sacks of grain into the mob. There were head-butts like the Rebs had never seen before — '*Ah'll lay the heed across ye, ye ignorant sassenach!*' — crunching noses, splitting foreheads, bruising knuckles and loosening teeth.

Many of the men unconsciously hesitated in delivering a blow, thrown off their stride by the kilts that were swirling about muscular legs, some giving glimpses of bare, pink buttocks: the overall impression was that they were about to punch a woman — and that hesitation cost many a spectator or re-enactment soldier some hide and blood.

There were only twenty Scotsmen

but they laid about them with such vigour and enthusiasm that the attackers were soon sprawled all over the ground like so many scattered skittle pins. Neither side escaped injuries but, luckily, no one resorted to weapons other than their fists or feet — or 'heeds'.

Captain Johnson organized a squad to break-up the fight and these men, tough regular soldiers from the fort, laid about it with a will, cracking heads and kicking butts, both kilted and trousered, until men fell back breathless, nursing their wounds, having lost all interest in continuing.

Matt Farrell, now wearing the plumed, wide-brimmed hat and other flamboyant regalia of a recreated Nathan Bedford Forrest, a much-loved Rebel General, sat his prancing palomino, waving his glittering sabre in the air. His beard had not yet grown fully but the stubble smudging his jowls did lend a certain toughness to his looks, thereby giving his words some extra weight.

'Stop this stupid brawling! You ought to be ashamed, all of you. Oh, I know you Scots were insulted and we apologize for that. You had a right to be riled, but, good Lord Almighty! Just look at what you've done! And it's not officially Battle Day until noon tomorrow!' He stood in the stirrups and called, 'First Aid squads! Do your work and be quick about it!'

Perhaps the uniform which every Confederate associated instantly with Forrest, helped, but whatever it was, men obeyed Farrell's commands and injuries were tended.

The spectators stood around, sullenly silent, feeling awkward, and then one tentatively asked if the Pipe Band could continue playing — *Scotland The Brave* or *The Skye Boat Song* or whatever other plaintive Highland tunes they had a mind to render. 'Drown out the Yankee accents with 'em!'

'Different kinda music to what we get here,' another added persuasively. 'An' we're gettin' used to the sound.'

It was the kind of thing Matt Farrell wanted to hear and he smiled at the battered drum major and his Scotsmen. 'Well, lads? It's their way of saying sorry — and that they like your music.'

'Och, weeellll,' said the major picking up his staff and examining the ornate silver capping for damage. 'What d'ye say, lads? Shall we give 'em *Scots Wha Hae*? Now there's a tune with a rebel touch, if ever I heard one.'

Matt Farrell silently blessed the man: it was just the thing that was needed to bring the Americans onside.

Although a bunch of Union soldiers, led by Lieutenant Joe Briscoe, standing watching the whole thing on a small ledge, almost started a fresh brawl.

'You hear that, boys?' jeered Big Joe. 'The Rebs are beggin' forgiveness! Beaten by a bunch of skirts! Hell, I always knew they was chicken-livered an' now we just seen the proof . . . '

There was a movement as a man in the uniform of a Yankee colonel, turned his mount and started away. Farrell narrowed his eyes: it was Colonel Kelvin Endicott Junior. Just by his presence, and now his exit, he had countenanced Briscoe's attempt to stir up trouble.

Captain Johnson and Farrell had to work mighty hard, but they managed to head-off another free-for-all and the band began playing through their repertoire, singing along with their fine Highland voices, the crowd's toes beginning to tap in time to the music and the rattle of the drums.

That night there were blazing camp-fires with everyone gathered around the draw, watching the Scots dance between crossed swords, big, clumsy-looking feet almost daintily expert. Later, they demonstrated tossing the caber, American eyes popping as the red-faced Scot who had hurled men bodily in the brawl upended an eight-foot log, sending it bouncing end over end twice with a single mighty heave.

'My God, that man is powerful,' allowed Farrell.

The drum major smiled. 'Aye, Wee Davey McTavish has muscles like the driveshaft of a steam engine.'

' 'Wee' — that means 'little', doesn't it?'

'Kind of an all-purpose word — but he was just a wee bairn. 'Tis the Hebridean porridge as makes 'em into men.'

'I dunno what that is, but Wee Davey's a fine example of what it can do,' Matt said, then excused himself: Winters was making his way slowly up the slope on foot. 'You missed some fine entertainment, Brad.'

'Heard some of it from down below — cattle did, too, and damned if they didn't seem to settle down to the sound of those pipes!' Winters took off his hat and mopped his forehead. 'We've moved the last cows well away. Thought we mightn't manage it before you started shooting off the cannons, but I reckon they'll be OK now.' He took the thick, leather-covered tallybook from his shirt pocket but Farrell waved it away, frowning a little.

'Not now, Brad. Too many things on my mind. Keep it till after the fireworks, or even till after the Battle — by the way, have you seen Banker Handy anywhere?'

'No.' Brad put the tallybook back in his shirt pocket, buttoned the flap. 'Is he supposed to be here?'

'Yes, I expected him by now. There's something a bit strange going on, Brad.' Farrell briefly told his foreman about the plan to ship out the huge amount of money in the bank safe to Denver by the train. 'Rather than leave it in the bank when the whole town'll be out here for Battle Day.'

'Sounds like a good notion,' Winters admitted.

'Well, I'm a little ashamed to say I felt uneasy enough about Ethan Handy saying Denver wouldn't agree that I checked at the telegraph office. Brad, Ethan Handy hasn't had any communication with the Denver Bank head office for several days.'

Brad frowned. 'What're you saying, Matt?'

'I don't even want to put it into words. But when I tried to see him last night after leaving the telegraph office, the bank was all in darkness. So I tried again this morning before I left for here to help set up the day's entertainment, but his wife — looking positively dreadful, all pale and strained — when she answered the door said the whole family had come down with some kind of food poisoning.' He waved a hand around to indicate the star-studded and music-filled darkness. 'Thought he would've made it by now, though.'

'Must still be too poorly,' opined Winters.

Matt Farrell shook his head. 'I checked with Doc Sawyer. He knows nothing about the Handy family coming down with food poisoning. Surely they would have contacted a sawbones for something as serious as that?'

Winters pursed his lips and shrugged. 'Bit strange — aw, you're not sending me in to check on him, I hope!'

Matt hesitated, then nodded in sudden decision. 'Would you mind, Brad? Find out what's keeping him, bring him back with you. Tell him I've reserved a tent and accommodation for all of his family so they can watch the show in comfort. I need him to help me run things. There're damn speeches, and he's more diplomatic than me with the Yankees. I need him out here badly, Brad.'

Winters nodded unenthusiastically and started to move away, knowing *he* might well be drafted in the banker's place if Farrell grew any more desperate. Then Matt called, 'You get your lieutenant's uniform I left on your bunk at the ranch?'

'Haven't had time to look in — not sure I'll even bother.'

'What about Endicott?'

Winters frowned slightly. 'What about him? It was his father, not him, who tortured Ryan.'

'He was out here a short time ago,

with Joe Briscoe and a bunch of Yankees trying to stir up trouble — I don't think he's quite finished with you yet, Brad.'

'Well, he better be. But he can come after me if he wants. I'll be waiting.'

Farrell's face hardened. 'Brad! You come back wearing that uniform! I've got big things planned for this show and I want to see you part of it — as Lieutenant Winters, just like old times. I want you to do this for me, Brad.'

Winters gave him a cool stare, not liking that 'for old times' sake' approach. Then, suddenly, he threw a snappy salute. 'Whatever you say, General.'

The words brought a smile to Farrell's face, but Brad was swearing quietly to himself as he made his way down the slope to where Kit Turner and some of the Block F crew were waiting for orders.

Goddamn stupid Battle Day! He'd had a bellyful already.

'Much more of this and I'll damn well quit!'

He wasn't aware that he had spoken aloud until he saw the startled faces of the waiting cowboys.

'What're you staring at? We got chores to do yet.'

10

Blood on the Saddle

Brad Winters took Kit Turner into town with him for no other reason than to have some company on the night ride. Kit wasn't all that pleased — he wanted to see what was going on at Hashknife, especially the fireworks, and definitely wanted to be there for the start of the re-enactment.

He had volunteered to take part in the battle and was looking forward to wearing a uniform again.

'Why aren't you keen on it, Brad?'

Winters shrugged. 'I dunno. From all accounts it was pretty much a slaughter and in my mind, don't much matter who won after all this time. Can't see how it 'honours the fallen' as Matt likes to say. A stone monument or a flagpole or something with their names on makes more sense to me.'

He sounded irritated and Kit decided to go easy.

'Yeah. But Matt's kind of found a place for himself, organizin' it all. *And* it's makin' the town a lot of money. Ranch, too, I guess.' Kit stifled a yawn as they came down out of the hills to the level stretch of trail that would eventually take them to town where very few lights still burned. 'Bunkhouse talk says Matt's aimin' to be Mayor of Hashknife and if this deal's a success he'll be elected easy.'

'That's just talk.' But Brad knew it could have some truth in it. Matt *was* more ambitious now the Block F was up and running. He shrugged. 'I really don't care one way or t'other. Guess I'll take part if that's what he wants.'

They were on the approaches to town now, Winters indicating they should take the creek trail. It would bring them out close to the bank building without having to make their way through Main and the side streets.

They splashed their mounts into the creek, belly deep, and were almost to the opposite bank when Winters reined-in sharply, stood in the stirrups. 'Who's that?'

Kit Turner followed Brad's pointing arm and saw a shadow slinking along the creek, crouching so that he kept the bushes between himself and the bank building.

Whoever it was heard the riders and they saw him start, hesitate, then plunge into the creek upstream. He waded swiftly towards the far bank. Winters spurred his mount along his side, cutting the man off as Kit rode up the creek, blocking any retreat.

Winters palmed up his six-gun. 'Stay put, feller!'

The man straightened, lifting his hands high. 'Hey, don't shoot! That you, Brad?' He spoke in a harsh whisper. 'It's only me — Boney Carson.'

Winters frowned, recognizing the youth now. He holstered his Colt as Turner halted his horse in the creek behind Boney. 'What you doin' slinkin' round here, kid?' Kit demanded.

Still standing thigh-deep in the water, Boney looked from one man to the other. 'Frog ain't around, is he?'

'Frog Delaney? No. But we're talkin' to you, kid.'

Boney swallowed and turned to Winters. 'I — I guess I can tell you. Mr Farrell's OK in my book, and you fellers work for him — '

'Get on with it, Boney,' Winters interrupted. 'What were you doing hanging around the bank?'

The youth licked his lips. 'I been hidin' out from Frog. He thinks I told the sheriff somethin' about him. I got hungry and ain't hardly anyone left in town. Mrs Handy sometimes gives me left-overs, so I came here and waited near the kitchen door. She sets out the garbage after they eat, or one of the gals does — but not tonight. I waited an' waited, belly growlin' . . . '

'Your ass is about to be kicked, Boney!' snapped Kit impatiently. 'Get on with it, boy!'

Boney looked alarmed, glanced wildly around and put a finger to his lips. 'Not so loud! They'll hear!'

'Who'll hear?' Winters asked quietly.

'The — the fellers in the bank with Mr Handy. I looked through a window when I smelled cookin' and there was these three fellers in the kitchen with Mr and Mrs Handy an' the gals. They had guns and they made the Handys stand agin the wall. That new gambler from Mooney's was there, too, guarded the Handys while Tibbetts and Griffin made Rona, the older daughter, bring 'em grub. Guess it'd be the gambler's turn to eat later.'

'You sure it was Tibbetts?' Brad asked quickly, and Boney nodded emphatically.

'Hell, yeah! I know Mort: run a few errands for him when he don't want to be seen by Sheriff Samson in town.' The youth paused, almost cringing, as if expecting a reprimand.

Winters glanced at Kit. 'Hostages.'

Kit nodded. 'No wonder Handy never showed up at Hashknife Ridge — guess they made him lie about Denver. And there was that story Mrs Handy told about food poisonin'.'

'Likely Tibbetts made Mrs Handy say that. Kit, you know what this looks like, don't you?'

'Damn right! They're holdin' the family hostage, and gonna make the banker open the safe!'

'That's it. And that gambler, Galvin, has joined-up with 'em — Gonna rob the bank while everyone's out at Hashknife Ridge watching the battle.'

'I s'pose you an' me gotta stop 'em, Brad.' Kit didn't sound enthusiastic at the prospect.

Winters turned to speak to Boney but the youth suddenly lunged for the creek bank, ducked past Brad's horse and ran into the bushes. Winters swore, started to call him back but cut off the words: if he yelled out, the thieves inside would hear. 'Kid's scared white!' he hissed. 'Better outa the way, I guess.

Looks like it's you and me, Kit. 'Less Samson left a couple of hired deputies in town.'

Just as he spoke there was a dull thud, followed by another, and rapid crackling sounds. They came from the direction of the distant Hashknife Ridge.

Rockets arced into the night sky, burst in small galaxies of blazing stars, followed by waves of smaller comets, and two huge mid-air explosions that lit up the hills with waves of fire. Spitting, whirling streaks of light flooded across the sky in great splashes of colour.

'What the hell's that?' Turner said, sounding awed.

'Matt's idea — loaded fireworks into the cannon, shot 'em off at the highest elevation, using the ridge slope as well to get a steeper angle. He wanted to make big explosions that could be seen from all over. Damnit, I told him it'll spook the herds or start a brushfire.'

'Sure is pretty though.'

Then the door at the rear of the bank

opened abruptly and a voice said, 'C'mon out, gals, and take a looksee — a little treat before we get down to the real business of the night, huh?' *Tibbetts.* 'Old Uncle Mort ain't so bad now, is he?'

While Tibbetts was speaking, Griffin pushed Ethan Handy's young daughters, Rona, seventeen, the other, Lila, fourteen, through the doorway. Tibbetts' voice suddenly became urgent. '*Someone's in the crick!*'

Tibbetts' gun came up blazing as he shoved the screaming girls back into the kitchen, shooting until his Colt was empty. 'Get 'em back inside, Reed!'

Griffin's gun blazed, too, and Kit, pistol drawn but as yet unfired, spurred away down the creek, water fanning outwards under his mount's hoofs. He jerked as two puffs of dust fluttered from his jacket. He was flung forward violently, but managed to stay in the saddle. He lost his grip on his six-gun and it splashed into the creek.

Winters threw himself sideways as

lead burned across his forearm, drawing blood, then dropped out of the saddle, taking his rifle with him. He jarred heavily and fumbled the working of the lever. A heavier gun thundered — Reed Galvin's Sheriff's Special — and turf and gravel kicked into the ramrod's face. He rolled swiftly down the slight slope of the bank, slewing around on his belly, triggered a trio of fast shots. Splinters flew from the door-frame, then he forced himself to hold his fire in case the women were in danger.

The hesitation gave Galvin a chance to steady his gun, grasping his wide wrist firmly with his left hand, the short barrel kicking as he triggered twice. Winters jarred as a bullet struck him somewhere high in the chest, the impact spinning him over the bank and into the creek.

Tibbetts, Colt reloaded now, and Griffin both turned their guns on Winters, shooting rapidly. Bullets zipped into the water around him, flailed turf and grit from the bank edge. He flung himself close in against the bank as Tibbetts yelled, 'Get that son of a bitch once and for all!'

He ran forward and Griffin followed, but Galvin paused and ran back into the bank to where the women cowered under the heavy kitchen table, the white-faced banker down on hands and knees trying to comfort them.

Griffin and Tibbetts ran along the bank as Winters kicked away into deeper water. But the splashing marked his position and Mort stopped, steadied his breathing and drew his bead. The Colt jumped as he fired the last shot in his cylinder. He whooped aloud as Winters' hat spun away and the man half-reared out of the water. The ramrod flopped back face down, and in the dim reflected glow from the fireworks, they saw the blood pouring down his face moments before his head submerged, something like red smoke puffing out around his hair.

'That's fixed the sonuver!' Griffin whooped.

'Make sure,' Tibbetts started to say, and paused as running footsteps brought him spinning around.

Two dark shapes, guns in their hands, skidded around the corner of the bank.

'The hell you doin', Mort?' one of the new arrivals demanded, panting. 'Thought this was s'posed to be a quiet deal!'

'A little unexpected trouble, Chip, but it's sorted out. OK, now you're *finally* here, you and Wiley go take care of the train crew. There's just the fireman and driver. Others are out at the fireworks show, I guess. Which suits us.'

Chip Durant let his gun swing casually in Tibbetts' direction. 'What'd suit me, is if you send Griffin with Wiley. I'll give you a hand with the cash.'

Tibbetts didn't like that but forced a grin. 'You been livin' in the Strip for too long, Chip . . . come on, then, let's go — Griff, go hold Wiley's hand.'

'OK, but someone better hold my share. *An'* damn tight!' Griffin said in a cold voice.

'Mine, too,' grated Wiley.

Tibbetts laughed briefly. 'Nice to see we all trust each other, ain't it? OK let's move.'

They separated and Brad Winters' body drifted, face down, away from the bank towards the short wooden bridge spanning the creek.

* * *

During the afternoon, Matt had arranged for the guns to be distributed to both sides. The weapons arrived in wagons driven by soldiers from the fort under Captain Johnson's supervision: rifles, pistols and bayonets. There were a lot of wooden practice bayonets included, but not as many as Farrell wished. He didn't want anyone getting seriously hurt, although he knew there would be inevitable casualties.

Two old enemies, recreating a savage

179

battle that had ended with victory for one and humiliation for the other — well, what could you expect? Tempers and old unresolved hostilities were bound to spring to the fore and take over in the heat of the moment. The hand-to-hand fighting and the bayonet charge by the Rebs would be the most dangerous times.

Farrell was in a real sweat now that Battle Day was fast aproaching. In 1864, it had actually started just before sundown, but as this would mean night-fighting and make it difficult for the spectators to see, the committee had agreed to bring the time forward to high noon. Matt seemed to be everywhere, checking this, criticizing that, making a note of something missing here. If he noted too much aggression in a particular squad, he ordered it to be broken up and the trouble-makers scattered throughout the rest of the Rebs or Yankees as the case may be.

There was still a lot of hostility between North and South and he could only try to keep it to a minimum during what he thought of now as *his* Battle Day.

When Captain Johnson reported that many of the Yankees were demanding real bayonets, refusing to use the wooden practice blades, Farrell climbed up onto the wagon distributing the bayonets, and somehow made himself heard over the catcalls and insults directed at him.

'Now get this straight: this is a *staged* action. A few men will be hurt, accidents being unavoidable, but any man who sets out to deliberately seriously injure an opponent will feel the full weight of the law! There'll be no leniency: it'll be jail, or a hangman's noose if anyone is killed . . . Now, think about that.'

His words sobered the men and the distribution of the bayonets went smoothly afterwards.

Farrell was regretting having sent Brad Winters into town after the banker. He could use a strong-willed, hard-fisted sidekick like Brad right now.

The next 'crisis' was Colonel Endicott, demanding that the blank ammunition be distributed before dark.

'My men — and I presume yours, too, Mr Farrell — will need time to get used to these old weapons. Many have used them of course, but we've had centre-fire ordnance and cartridges for over ten years now. It's going to look very strange, if not downright comical, if our men go into battle and can't fire their weapons without fumbling.'

Matt didn't like Endicott. He had met him on several occasions, each time complaining about something that didn't suit him: the food, the campsite, the river water, the quality of the tent he had been assigned, the language of the Rebs, even the consistency of his boot polish. As the petty complaints lengthened, Matt felt a rising hostility. The man was so obviously a product of the snobbish West Point: arrogant, self-opinionated, insisting he get his own way, right or wrong, eyes focused on personal glory.

Now, he met the cold, arrogant stare of Kelvin Endicott Junior, with steady gaze. He could well believe the man's sire had ordered the sadistic torture of young Ryan Winters. Before him stood a man with a pathological hatred of all things Southern. He could barely force himself to speak with a civil tongue. But Matt was no pushover.

'Colonel, I'll concede that the men need a little practice with muzzle-loaders, but that's all been arranged for the morning — a couple of hours ought to be enough, and then we can start the battle at noon as planned.'

'A couple of hours!' cut in the colonel, his young, bitter face colouring deeply. 'I believe you *want* my men to look foolish! Is that it, Farrell? You've devised an exercise in humiliation? Good God, man! D'you really think it matters that we lost one piddling battle? *We won the War!*'

Farrell shook his head briefly. 'And are forever reminding us of it. But, if you feel that way, Colonel, you shouldn't be in charge of your contingent.'

'You damn glory-seeker! You're getting way beyond yourself, Farrell! I'm a full Colonel in the Army of the United States of America and — '

'At present, a guest of Hashknife County, Colorado Territory, soon to be admitted to the Union as a fully fledged State.' Matt was weary of the man's smug superiority. 'Familiarization with the firearms will take place at nine tomorrow morning, in Kicking Horse Gulch. I'll see you there.'

He wheeled and strode away before Endicott could reply, seething — and with not a little apprehension knotting his belly. *Would the man be loco enough to try something really foolish?*

But his tension eased when the fireworks display went off better than he had dared hope. It was received with rowdy enthusiasm and approval by the spectators.

Then a voice called from near the

Scotsmen's camp just after the last of the cannons' fiery blasts.

Wee Davey McTavish bellowed loudly for Matt.

'Mr Farrell! We'd be pleased if ye cud c'mon doon here for a moment, sir. We have a laddie ridin' a fine piece of horseflesh he admits doesna belong to him — and there be blood on the saddle.'

Then Spud Bromley, already running down to the Scots' camp, skidded to a halt, muttered a curse and called, 'Matt! It's Brad's buckskin! An' Boney Carson's in the saddle lookin' like Old Nick's about three feet behind him an' comin' up fast!'

11

The Train

Banker Ethan Handy was shaking, sick deep down in his stomach. These men who were standing around as if they owned his residential section of the bank building frightened him out of his socks.

To his credit, his fear wasn't just for his own hide: he was concerned about his wife, who never was a hundred per cent healthy, and, of course, his two lovely daughters. They were at the edge of full-flowering womanhood; Lila, the youngest at fourteen, showing a figure almost as full as that of her seventeen-year old sister, Rona.

Handy saw the way the gunmen leered at them, but he knew their lust would not stop there if they allowed themselves to indulge it. Even his wife wouldn't be safe.

He was, by now, familiar with Tibbetts, also Reed Galvin, the sullen gambler. The other man, the one they called Chip, was dirty, smelled of wild trails and had a habit of running his tongue around inside his bottom lip that made Handy want to smash a chair over his head. Several remarks he had overheard told him that Chip had come across specially from the Cherokee Strip with his sidekick, Wiley, to help with the bank robbery — and the getaway. Wiley apparently was an ex-railroad man and knew how to drive a locomotive.

Now the moment Ethan Handy dreaded had arrived.

Tibbetts made the three women sit on the floor with their backs to the wall near the stove, hands clasped around their knees and voluminous skirts. They huddled together, shoulder to shoulder, seeking strength and reassurance from each other by the slight touching of their bodies. Their eyes were large as they watched every movement the gunmen made.

Mort Tibbetts now stood in front of the sweating, sallow-faced banker. He jerked his head towards the womenfolk.

'Nice-lookin' family, you got, banker — specially the young'uns, but your wife ain't all that old and she's holdin' up pretty good in the looks department, eh?'

Handy swallowed, knew he wasn't expected to say anything, but he did, anyway, meaning it as a small comfort to the women. 'They are all very dear to me — please don't harm them.'

Tibbetts stared a moment without expression, then grinned, glanced at Chip Durant and Galvin. 'Now ain't that nice? Good ol' poppa tryin' to act brave in front of his family.'

'We're wasting time, Mort,' Reed Galvin said, and he didn't flinch at the bleak look Tibbetts directed at him. 'A couple of minutes wasted here means a half-mile along the track we haven't covered.'

'Din' have you down as a 'fraidy-cat, Reed, not after the way you downed them card-sharps.'

'Being careful is not being afraid, Mort.'

Chip Durant growled, 'He's right, Mort. Let's get movin'. I don't like towns.'

'Told you you'd been too long in the Strip. OK. Banker, you know what we want. You're the only one can open the safe, right? You ain't gonna gimme trouble, are you?'

Handy glanced at the terrified women. 'I-I can't!' He was speaking to them rather than the robbers. 'I-I've always prided myself on acting in the bank's best interests — *My God! Get away from them!*'

Tibbets was standing threateningly over the women now. Handy started forward but Reed Galvin reached out casually with his left hand, sank hard fingers into the banker's shoulder, and flung him back against the wall. Then Galvin hit him in the belly with the side of his six-gun. The banker gagged and doubled over.

Lila screamed, started to rise, but sank back swiftly as Rona touched her arm. 'Don't let them frighten you, Lila,'

Mrs Handy's lips were moving and her eyes were upturned as she prayed silently, hands clasped.

Tibbetts grinned crookedly at the sagging banker. 'I forgot to tell you, Banker, you only get one chance — but I'll bend my own rules just this once: you gonna open that safe?'

Handy was almost crying as he looked at his family, but swallowed, looked Tibbetts in the eye and shook his head.

Without looking away, Tibbetts said, 'Chip, take your pick.'

Handy collapsed to a sitting position as Durant moved across to where the women sat, picked his nose as he studied them one by one. The outlaw reached down towards Lila, paused, then leered at the banker, changed direction and twisted his fingers in the long blonde tresses of Rona. She cried out as he started to lift her, hands going up to snatch at Durant's wrist so her hair wouldn't be pulled out of her scalp. Mrs Handy wrapped her arms about one of Chip's legs, trying to upset him. Young Lila cowered away as far as she could. Then Ethan Handy spoke as Durant lifted a threatening hand, the words almost choking him.

'Stop! Stop for God's sake! I'll do it!'

'Father, no!' gasped Rona, as Durant released her and she sat down again heavily, rubbing her stinging scalp. 'All that money people have paid! You can't let this . . . rabble have it.'

Tibbetts dragged the banker to his feet by the arm. He leaned down close to Rona. 'Now you shut up, sis! An' that goes for you other ladies, too! You try anythin' and — '

He shook the banker and Rona said defiantly, 'What will you do? Kill him? Then how would you get the safe open?'

191

'Oh, I ain't stupid; I'd shoot your old man, all right. But only put a slug through his foot or his knee, might even bust a hand with my gun butt . . . or I could start on you an' your sister and ma. Hell, there's lots of ways I can make a man do what I want. Know what I mean, sis?'

'Shut your filthy mouth!' snapped Handy and reeled as Tibbetts back-handed him, splitting his lip.

'Now, now, Pa, don't you get so excited. The boys here'll stay with the ladies while you and me go into the bank and take a looksee at that safe — OK?'

He grabbed the banker by the back of his collar, propelled him violently through the doorway into the passage that led to the bank itself.

Reed Galvin put one boot up on the stove and leaned an arm across his knee, face deadpan. Chip Durant went and stood over Rona, scratching thoughtfully at the stubble on his chin. Mrs Handy fainted.

* * *

Down at the rail depot, Wiley and Griffin made their way to the caboose at the end of the siding where a lamp glow was visible through the open door. As they drew closer, watching the locomotive and its other passenger cars, not yet hitched up or occupied, they heard low voices from inside.

'Never seen fireworks like that before, Milt.'

'Me, neither. Them big blasts in the sky — *woo-hoo!* Wish I was up there on the ridge.'

'No chance. We might see some of the Battle Day, though, if we slow down after the horsehoe bend.'

'Or, if we're early enough, we can try to find a hoss. Not that I like ridin', been ridin' a footplate too long.'

'Hey! That sounds good!'

'No it don't!' a harsh voice snapped. 'When you get this rust-bucket rollin', you don't stop till we tell you.'

The railroad men, sitting at their

ease, sipping from a flat flask of whiskey, jumped to their feet as Wiley and Griffin leapt up through the caboose doorway, waving their guns. Griffin didn't waste any time: he slammed the smaller man, Milt, across the head with his Colt, knocking him halfway across the caboose to fall amongst some parcels, scalp bleeding, barely conscious.

The other one, taller and younger, named Buzz, lifted his hands to protect himself, but Wiley stepped in and kneed him brutally in the crotch. The man fell writhing.

Milt was moaning, holding his bleeding head. Buzz looked up with contorted face, hands buried deep between his legs.

'Which of you is the engineer?' Wiley asked and kicked Buzz in the side. 'Quick!'

Buzz, gasping, a little vomit on his lips, now, nodded towards Milt. 'OK, now listen, when he comes round we're gonna hitch up the caboose and the passenger cars to the loco.'

Buzz frowned, but nodded, still in great pain.

'Then you're gonna take me, my friends an' some of our — baggage' — Wiley winked at Griffin — 'just where we tell you. No arguments, savvy?'

Buzz looked alarmed even through his pain. 'We ain't s'posed to leave till the show's over at Hashknife Ridge.'

'That so?' Wiley said. 'Well, just get used to the notion, mister, that we're in charge and callin' the shots.'

'We'll be leavin' in about an hour,' Griffin told him and Buzz looked wide-eyed alarmed. Griffin stood over him, boot raised threateningly. 'What the hell you lookin' like that for?'

'We ain't even got a head of steam on.'

'What's he talkin' about?' Griffin asked Wiley.

'Boiler's cold, has to be fired-up to pressure.'

'Well, get him started on it!'

'Might take *hours!*' Wiley replied, looking worried. 'We could still be here come daylight!'

'Cherrrist!' Griffin kicked Buzz again, brutally. 'Might be a lot of townsfolk who only went to see the fireworks come back to stay in town over night, too!'

Wiley nodded gloomy agreement. 'And we might still be sitting here, knee-deep in all that cash, with the safe standing open and empty. And the train not ready to roll.'

Griffin cocked his pistol and rammed the muzzle against Buzz's head. The railroad man hunched his shoulders and closed his eyes tightly, expecting to die.

'Mister, you get that steam pressure up before daylight or you'll never see another goddamn sunrise. I guarantee it!'

* * *

Boney Carson didn't like being the centre of attention. Usually when that happened it was because he was in trouble. But Matt Farrell spoke to him calmly and frowned at Sheriff Samson who was inclined to bully the youth.

'Just take it easy, Boney, tell us what's happened and how come you're riding Brad Winters' horse.'

His voice a little shaky at first, but gathering strength as he got into the swing of things, Boney told the men gathered around and hanging on his every word what he had seen in Hashknife.

'Just bad luck Tibbetts and his men come out to see the fireworks, Mr Farrell. Soon's they spotted Brad and Kit they started shootin' and I lit-out into the brush.'

'We need to know about Winters and Turner,' Samson snapped impatiently.

'Both — dead.' Boney gulped and looked worriedly around as the group was gripped by total silence. Clearing his throat, he added, 'While Tibbetts and Griffin went back into the bank, I grabbed Brad's hoss when it come runnin' to me an' lit-out to tell Mr Farrell here.'

'Bastards are robbin' the bank!' the

197

sheriff growled. 'We'd better get into town pronto.'

Farrell, mouth dry, his chest tight and stomach churning at the news that Brad was dead, said quietly, 'Someone'll have to go get some horses then.'

Several men moaned: they had momentarily forgotten that all the horses had been driven up into the hills and turned loose in natural holding canyons, far enough away from Knife Edge so the fireworks wouldn't frighten them and set them running wild.

Farrell heaved a sigh. 'Well, someone better start walking. Brad's mount's wore out, no sense in killing it by trying to race him through these hills in the dark.'

'Be lucky if we get a posse on the trail by sun-up!' Slade Samson said, in his usual gloomy tones.

'Yankees might've kept their hosses,' Spud Bromley said. 'Endicott said he wasn't gonna trust no Rebs to look after his 'fine Northern stock'.'

Sheriff Samson took out his Colt and spun the chamber slowly, checking the loads. 'We'll talk to him first.'

For once, Matt Farrell didn't mind the lawman taking charge.

* * *

The Yankee camp was a mess.

They had kept their mounts instead of taking advice and sending them off to the canyons where they would not be frightened by the fireworks.

The horses panicked even when the first small rockets streaked skyward and spread falling stars across the heavens. Then there came the big cannon shots, with the whistling, screaming shells that burst like thunderclaps.

Naturally, in their fear, the picketed animals wrenched out their line ropes and ground pegs and *ran*. They thundered wildly through the lines of tents, wrecking and shredding them all, scattering the occupants, smashed cooking areas, rifle stacks and everything else in their path.

Farrell could hardly keep a straight face as he asked Colonel Endicott if there were any mounts at all they might borrow. 'Or are you still trying to round 'em up?'

'Just get the hell out of my camp!' Endicott was not a happy man, riled at what he saw as a fresh humiliation. 'Can't you see how busy we are straightening up!'

Farrell and the sheriff chuckled as they made their way back to the other side of the ridge to Knife Edge. But they still didn't have horses to ride . . .

By the time Spud and his helpers finally got back with half-a-dozen mounts, sun-up wasn't far off.

Most of the picked posse-men saddled swiftly and rode for town, but Matt reluctantly decided he had better stay to organize the battle which would have to go on as advertised at any cost.

So he missed the excitement and astonishment as the posse, coming down towards the flats that surrounded the town, heard three spaced gunshots coming from a stand of timber.

The sheriff thought he heard a distant sound like a train whistle, but he had no time to confirm it as a ragged, bloody figure staggered into view, a smoking six-gun held down at his side. It was Kit Turner, barely able to stand, one arm dangling, dried blood on his ragged sleeve, more smeared across his face. Men rushed towards him but he collapsed before they reached him.

He came round while they tended the bullet wound in his left upper arm and the shallow groove cut across his back. He told them how he and Brad had been jumped in the creek behind the bank, gasping over each word.

'They just winged me, but it skewed me in the saddle and the hoss tossed his head, busted my nose — was all I could do to hang on. But I seen Brad get hit and he went into the creek, face down in the water — current carried him downstream, towards the town bridge.'

He shook his head, mouth grim.

'He's dead, for sure. I musta passed out. When I came round, the train was just leavin' with both passenger cars and the caboose.'

'It wasn't due to leave till after Battle Day,' the sheriff growled.

'Well, it's gone now. Dunno who's aboard, but I reckon Tibbetts and his pards are, with the money from the bank. I found Brad's Colt near the creek an' spotted you fellers just as I was gonna see what'd happened to Handy and his family.'

Samson looked around at the others: everyone was grim-faced. 'Let's do that now,' he said, without much enthusiasm.

It was clear he didn't think they'd be found alive.

12

Decoy

Brad Winters almost drowned after the bullet seared across his scalp, sending his hat flying. It snapped his head back and hurt his neck, twisting his body so that he was face down in the sluggish creek.

His chest was tight and aching and he knew he had been hit high up. He managed to snatch a partial breath — it hurt too much for him to drag down a really deep one.

The current moved him slowly, taking him away from the others, towards the wooden bridge that connected the two parts of the town: residential on one side, business on the other. Lungs bursting, he reached down and found he could just manage to pull himself along by his fingertips. Luckily, the robbers had other things on their minds. The shooting stopped and his blurring brain decided they must have returned to the bank and the hostages. *Well, right now, there was nothing he could do about that . . . .*

His head ached and he felt nauseous. The bridge was drawing closer. Feebly, he grabbed at a piling but it was too slippery. His body banged into another, half curling around it, His chest was on fire. Strong bursts of pain surged through him with each movement. The stars were dimming, one by one, and he knew he was passing out, and that he had better find shallow water or he would drown. Blackness claimed him, deep, dead blackness — finally turning slowly, so very slowly, to grey.

Probably the cold water lapping his face brought him back to consciousness enough so he could crawl onto a muddy slope and draw up his legs. He was still beneath the bridge and only half-aware, lying there, huddled, trying to make the world stop bouncing around. The darkness coming and going seemed to take a long time to settle into a uniform greyness. Only later did he recognize this as the new day gradually approaching. Soon the sun would appear over Hashknife.

More or less settled down at last, he took stock of his position. The groove in his scalp above the left ear was not deep but he was lucky to be alive — a little closer and it would have taken the side of his head off. Next, he felt gingerly for the chest wound — but there was no wound. The thick leather-covered tally book Matt had insisted he keep with him had deflected the bullet, but the impact had left a bruise the size of his hand.

He was near Bede Halstrom's store, now in darkness and locked up. Swaying, unsteady on his feet, Winters looked back towards the bank building again. Lights were showing at the windows, and vague shadows that could be men moving about.

Dizziness swept over him, blood still

oozing from his scalp wound. When he steadied, he felt again his sodden, filthy clothes — and the empty holster. Weaving and staggering he found his way to the rear of Halstrom's store. He was prepared to bust the door open by any means he could manage, but someone had beaten him to it. The door sagged inward at his touch.

Warily, weaponless, he slid inside and along a wall, but his senses told him he was alone here. In the dim light, he stripped and towelled himself dry and reasonably clean. While he was doing this he heard a brief whistle from the locomotive and, dimly, the clank of couplings as the train started moving. *He bet the thieves were on board!*

He fumbled for clothing on the low shelves. He tripped and fell sprawling. The whistle screamed again, a banshee in the night. Lying on his back, struggling to pull on a pair of corduroy trousers, Winters froze, head cocked as he listened, puzzled.

It sounded like a bunch of horses was

crossing the bridge, hoofs rattling hollowly on the timber planks! *But if Tibbetts and his men were on the train, who could be riding? It must be mounts from the livery pens, frightened by the whistle blast, no one around to stop them kicking down the rails and running off . . . .*

He finished dressing, went to the street window but could see nothing. So he broke the glass on the gun cabinet, took a Colt, and fresh ammuntiion, an Ithaca shotgun, and loaded it, too. Next, he grabbed a bottle of whiskey from a cupboard that had already been forced open, and gulped down a couple of mouthfuls: its warmth spread through him, gave him extra strength that he badly needed.

Figuring there was nothing to lose now, he made his way through to the front of the store and the street door. He passed the big storage cupboard where the spare re-enactment uniforms were kept, surprised to find the doors wide open and the uniforms scattered

207

all over the floor. Candy jars were broken open, too, and the tobacco shelf held only two sacks of the makings now. Some canned food rolled about the uneven floor, making him stumble. He shook his head briefly.

There was always someone willing to loot and plunder if the opportunity offered. A bullet was too good for 'em.

Going warily onto the boardwalk, shotgun held ready, he wondered what he was going to find at the bank, but didn't allow his thoughts to dwell too long on it.

Once the banker had opened the safe, the hostages would be of no further use to the thieves. In fact, they would be a liability, could too easily identify them.

And there was only one way to ensure that didn't happen . . .

But he was pleasantly surprised when he found the entire Handy family bound and gagged, in the parlour but still very much alive.

After he had untied them, while the

womenfolk had a little weep of relief and comforted each other, Ethan Handy, pale and visibly shaken, told Winters, 'Wiley, Chip Durant and Griffin wanted to kill us. Tibbett would've gone along with the idea, but that gambler, Galvin, said if they killed a whole family of innocents, the law would tear the country apart looking for them and would never give up. They'd be on the run forever.'

'He's right. Tibbetts is no fool. He would've seen that.'

'Thank God he did! Brad, they've taken the train. They'll be well on the way to Denver and their escape by the time you can get to Slade Samson and organize a posse.'

'Been thinking about that.' Winters leaned a hip against the table, not wanting to show he was still not fully in control of his faculties. 'Need a horse, Ethan. If I go by way of Pitsaw Bluff, I can cut across to the horsehoe bend where the rail tracks force the train to slow down — '

'Brad! You're one man! A wounded one at that! And these are killers!'

'And getting away with all that money they stole from your bank, Ethan.'

He didn't think it possible for Handy to go any whiter but the man did, his shoulders sagging. 'Of course, you're right.' He hesitated, wrung his hands and said tightly, 'All right, take my Arab. It's in the stables out back. I'll send Rona out to Hashknife to warn the sheriff.'

But Brad was already hurrying out the door into the fast-lightening morning.

* * *

The Arab stallion was all black, sleek and slim in the fashion of its breed. It had been Ethan Handy's pride and joy for the last couple of years, and Rona, the only other one of his family who enjoyed riding, had her own mount, a high-bred Appaloosa. Handy often boasted he had a small fortune invested in those mounts.

None of which mattered a damn to Brad Winters as he rode the big black through the beginning day, coming out of the shadow of Pitsaw Bluff and into a stretch of sage and sotol. Far beyond this he could see the black, oily brush-stroke of the train's smoke. It seemed to be making good speed. He could see a glowing curved thread out there: the giant silver horseshoe, where the rails skirted suspect land that had once been a swamp. The railroad hadn't been prepared to risk running track straight across, so took the longer, but safer way, and curved their rails around the area. To save distance — and rails — they had made the horseshoe sharper than originally planned so that trains were forced to slow down on the actual curve until they hit the straight again.

It was this enforced change of speed Winters was counting on to give him time to reach the train before it began to accelerate once more. He was feeling better by the minute, but the thought of swinging aboard that train with four or five cold-blooded killers waiting did not excite him.

All he could do was hope that Rona Handy reached Sheriff Samson quickly and the lawman would come hell-for-leather with a posse before Brad was riddled by Tibbetts and his men.

The Arab responded well but wasn't used to prolonged running and was beginning to falter, streaming with sweat.

'C'mon, hoss! Keep going! Make Ethan proud of you!'

Crazy! Talking to a dumb animal now! But sometimes just the sound of an encouraging human voice urged the mount to greater effort — better than a jab with spurs.

He wouldn't say his words had any noticeable effect on the big black but they did seem to cross the brush at a good speed. They came to the low hogback between him and the train.

Warily, he dismounted below the crest, kept hold of the reins, not trusting the panting black to stay put without some restraint. The bruised chest muscles made him wince as he looked over cautiously. He started, half-rearing up, not believing what he was seeing.

The train was slowed in the deep curve as expected, but what was not expected was the sight of a man jumping from the caboose into the brush as the train moved slowly past and began to gather speed again as it entered the beginning of the straight.

Not only that, the man picked himself up and ran into a nearby small stand of timber. Minutes later, with the train now speeding away along the straight track, the man appeared, riding a big chestnut horse that he spurred towards the distant Hashknife Ridge.

★ ★ ★

The man who had jumped from the train was Wiley.

Only minutes earlier he had climbed out of the engine cab, over the piled tender of split log firewood. He had been riding up front with Buzz and Milt since the train had left Hashknife siding. He held a cocked six-gun in his hand, making the train crew nervous as they cleared town and, at his orders, piled on the speed.

'All right,' he said after a time. 'Keep it goin' flat out.'

'We got the horseshoe comin' up soon,' Milt cautioned nervously.

'I know it!' snapped Wiley, looking as if he would pistol-whip Milt. 'Do what you have to do, but just keep this train movin' till I tell you different. Now, I'm goin' back to my friends in the caboose but I'll be along from time to time to check. When you come outa the horseshoe, you pile it on, fast as this old rust-bucket will take.'

He flicked the gun barrel warningly and both men flinched. Milt opened the throttle a little more with a hand that trembled. Buzz threw two more logs into the firebox.

Wiley made his way back confidently towards the caboose along the tops of the swaying, empty passenger cars. He climbed down the short ladder onto the forward landing of the caboose but made no attempt to enter. He stayed there until the train slowed and began to make its laborious way around the horseshoe bend.

Then he moved to the outer side, knowing Milt and Buzz would be naturally watching the inside curve as the train progressed towards the straight track beyond.

Wiley even smiled as he jumped into the brush, rolled and lay there briefly to allow the train to gather speed and move well away before he ran to his waiting horse tethered in the stand of timber.

As he mounted, he laughed out loud, wishing he could see the faces of those two idiots in the cab when they finally stopped and realized they had been busting their back, thrashing an empty train along for the last few hours. Wiley spurred his chestnut away from the trees and headed for the line of ragged ranges.

He ran the chestnut into a draw that was the start of the mountains that rose steeply to Hashknife Ridge. His heart jumped into his throat and he reined down sharply, reaching for his six-gun, as soon as he saw the rider on the big, sweating black Arab, blocking the trail.

A shotgun lifted as Brad Winters called, 'Don't touch it, Wiley!'

But Wiley had been reacting instinctively in such situations for so long that he couldn't have stopped himself drawing that Colt if he had wanted to. He was a man used to self-preservation and he was already throwing himself sideways out of the saddle, Colt blasting.

The speed of the man's draw caught Brad by surprise and he ducked instinctively as lead whined past, automatically triggering the Ithaca shotgun. The blast startled the Arab and it reared, whinnying, pawing the air with those slim, muscular forelegs, unseating the ramrod.

When he hit, he lost the shotgun, but wasted no time trying to retrieve it. He rolled fast, not even feeling the tearing pain across his chest. His hat jarred off and the pad of folded calico it had been holding in place on the scalp wound fell away. He was not consciously aware of any of these things as Wiley's next two bullets kicked gravel into his face. His own Colt was in his hand now and he fired as Wiley jumped up and ran for the shelter of a rock. The Arab ran across, spoiling Winters' aim, but it made Wiley pause, too, so as to avoid being run down.

Brad thumbed the hammer twice and, although the gun was new and neither oiled nor tuned very well, they were very fast shots, the second driving hard on the heels of the first. They brought Wiley down, smashing into his moving body, adding their impact so that he twisted violently, legs folding, sending him crashing face down.

He did not move except for one leg, which twitched three or four times before becoming still.

Brad used a boot toe to turn the man over, saw the chest, smashed and bloody. He squatted, looking into the outlaw's glazing eyes.

'Time for a few words before you go, Wiley. OK?'

13

Battle Day

If Wee Davey McTavish hadn't drawn
the short straw and so had to make the
pipe-and-drum band's breakfast porridge that morning, history might well
have been changed by the Battle at
Hashknife Ridge, 1879.

Davey was a big — huge! — easy-
going lad and hummed *My Bonnie
Lassie* as he collected firewood and
stacked it beside the big hemispherical
iron pot of oatmeal already bubbling
over flames within a rock circle. He
threw in a handful of salt, stirred, then
stretched his massive muscles, placing
his hands in the small of his back,
easing a little stiffness from sleeping out
of doors: the night had held a lot more
chill than he had expected. As he did,
still humming, he looked around,

enjoying the beauty of early morning as peach-coloured sunlight gradually washed down the side of the hills and through the campsite. It picked out the details of green and rust-hued leaves, a few flowers, the splash of coloured bird wings — and the sudden, eye-squinting flash of *something!*

He strained to see what had winked so brilliantly below there near the path that led to the Yankees' camp. There were several other flashes as he watched and suddenly, hard on a whispered oath, his stentorian voice bellowed,

'Wake up, ye great snortin' lumps of haggis! Yankees are comin' up the glen!'

He snatched up his pipes from where they rested near the door of his tent, hurriedly blew air into the tartan-covered bladder, and squeezed out a note that cut through the morn like the cry of a dying gull. Within seconds the rousing strains of *Scotland The Brave* wafted across the slopes of Knife Edge Camp. The drummer, staggering in just his kilt, beat *To Quarters!* on his kettle drum, the raw, rattling sound bringing cries of protest as sleepy-eyed, dishevelled figures stumbled out of their tents.

'You goddamn crazy Scotsmen! What the hell's all this racket — *Oh, Jesus! It's a raid! The blue-bellies are makin' a goddamn sneaky raid!'*

The Yankees, discovered now, and knowing there was little they could do but try to keep whatever advantage they still held, let out a roar, a mixture of battle cries and insults, and charged. They ran through the trees and up the slopes with bayonets fixed to their long muskets, mounted officers flashing sabres.

Big Joe Briscoe urged the men on. 'Remember the colonel's orders, boys: Burn the tents! Capture the cannon! Crack those rebel skulls! *Victory to the Union! No quarter!'*

Caught off-guard, some tents already ablaze or torn down, men struggling to get out from under collapsing canvas, the Confederates strived to clear their buzzing heads and meet the enemy.

Rallying rebel yells tore the morning apart. Musket fire rattled raggedly, sending choking clouds of powdersmoke drifting through the camp and the struggling men. Wooden practice bayonets clashed with the real thing, broke or splintered. A couple of men were cut deeply and slashed. Incensed, the Rebs fought back with crushing rifle butts, fists and elbows, even clubs and stones. No punches were pulled by either side.

Bones cracked, noses bled, teeth were spat all over the slopes. There was a craziness abroad in Hashknife Ridge that morning: men acted as if this was the original battle, with the only object to kill or maim as many of the enemy as possible. Overwhelming enthusiasm and long-restrained passions, resentments and hatreds took charge.

Aroused spectators lined the slopes, mostly half-dressed or some still in night attire, cheering or booing, depending on their preferences. Many hurled rocks at the Yankees, incensed at the treacherous attack.

Because of the rogue raid at first light instead of six or seven hours later at noon, the Rebs had been caught napping and, though fighting valiantly, were forced to retreat slowly, step-by-step, as the blue uniforms swarmed across the slope. Someone noted, aloud and with suitable epithets, that there seemed to be a hell of a lot more than one hundred blue-bellies wrecking the camp.

Right now, the fight was distinctly one-sided, all the weight with the Yankee hordes.

The Scotsmen, because they had elected to camp near the Confederate lines, were considered legitimate targets by the Union soldiers. Riled-up, the kilted men abandoned their pipes and drums — although three stood guard to see the instruments came to no harm — and turned to meet the attackers, reinforcing the Rebs' scattered forces.

Once Wee Davey saw there was no quarter, asked or given, he snatched up his heavy ladle, laid about him briefly, then scooped dollops of steaming oatmeal into the red faces of the yelling Yankees. He grabbed a waistband here and there, pouring the still bubbling mash down the front of heavy blue trousers. The screams and frantic dancing about disrupted many a brawl, tripped lunging men.

When the big iron pot was more than half empty, Wee Davey grabbed the edges with a rag in each hand and hurled the massive vessel bodily into a line of attackers. There were cries of pain and the line broke as the weighty iron pot wobbled and thundered erratically down the slope, men dodging desperately, both blue and grey. Not all escaped the thundering drunken juggernaut.

This rout gave the Rebels a chance to rally and regroup on that part of the slope. They charged after the fleeing Yanks, pistols popping, some muskets with fixed steel bayonets, yelling insanely.

The entire slope was shrouded in billowing gunsmoke, ghostly figures weaving in and out, struggling groups revealed here and there. Mounted Yankees raced through the action, used their mounts to advantage, knocking down men who didn't get out of the way in time. Sometimes an over-zealous naked sabre whistled down and laid bare Rebel bones beneath bloody flesh.

Everyone was bellowing something and if there were specific orders they were unintelligible, lost in the general din. A few Rebs loaded one of the cannon, fired it into a group of Yankees determinedly struggling up the slope. They reeled and choked as a jetting column of powdersmoke enshrouded them, stinging, burning, blinding. If the gun had been primed with grapeshot, the slope would have been a butcher's shop.

The Reb team sweated and stumbled over themselves, trying to reload. But a new bunch of Yankees swarmed in from upslope, beat about them relentlessly, and overturned the heavy gun. It tumbled down the slope in murderous, uncontrolled bounces. Running men scattered as it careered down slope, jarring so hard that the barrel broke free of the carriage. One of the wheels splintered against rocks, the spokes shattering.

The action served only to infuriate the already raging Confederates and there was a vicious clash between the groups. The way two men fell — loose-limbed, bloody-faced, whites of eyes showing — it seemed as if there would be some really serious casualties before this battle was over.

Matt Farrell, wearing only part of his Nathan Bedford Forrest uniform, but with his feathered hat in place, tried to rally his men as they were gradually overwhelmed by greater numbers of Union soldiers.

'Hold your ground, men! Don't let Yankee foul play win!'

He jerked his head as roiling gunsmoke suddenly wreathed his face. He coughed, eyes stinging. Big Joe Briscoe gave him a mocking smile, smoking pistol in hand.

'Even blanks can hurt, eh, Reb? Try this!'

He fired the big Dragoon Colt close to Matt's face. The jet of smoke blinded Farrell and the explosion deafened him. He staggered, disoriented, and Briscoe gun-whipped him.

'Forrest's down!' he bellowed, standing with one foot on the semi-conscious Farrell. 'You've lost your leader, Rebs! Surrender, or we'll wipe you out!'

'No!' Matt roared inside his swirling brain. 'It's not meant to be this way . . .'

'Surrender, I say!' Briscoe bawled again.

'Like hell!' Sheriff Slade Samson, face beet red, sweaty shirt in tatters, his game leg dragging, stumbled in and swiped the peaked felt cap from the startled Briscoe's head. Then the lawman reversed his hold on his Colt and smashed the butt between Big Joe's eyes. The man dropped like a sack of wet grain.

The sheriff knelt beside the semi-conscious Farrell, shook him by the shoulder, keeping an eye on the fighting going on around them.

'Matt! Matt! I've just heard Brad's alive! I missed him in town, but Rona Handy told me he's gone after the train — Tibbetts and his crew are on board with the money. They've cut the telegraph wires so we'll have to form a posse and go after 'em . . .'

Matt was unable to take it all in in his present state but as he looked up, kind of vaguely, a mounted Yankee rode in, swinging his sabre, leaning far out of the saddle to make his strike. Slade Samson staggered as the blade hacked across his left arm, high up near the shoulder, laying open a bloody wound.

Colonel Endicott seemed a little startled at what he had done: obviously his blood was up and he was carried away somewhat with the general fighting. His horse pranced and he yanked the reins one-handed. Then a second rider slammed into him, full-tilt, and sent him flying out of the saddle. Both mounts went down in a tangle, whickering and thrashing wildly.

Dazed, Endicott staggered up, saw his sword lying on the ground and lunged for it. A bullet smashed into the blade, shattering it and sending the two parts skidding in different directions. The colonel leapt back, rounded angrily — but froze as he looked into the smoking muzzle of Brad Winters' Colt.

'You — you're using real bullets!' Endicott accused, outraged, but with a touch of fear in his voice and wary eyes.

'You're lucky I didn't put one through you.' Brad shifted his gaze to Samson as the man fumbled a neckerchief over the arm wound. 'All right, Slade?'

'Yeah. What the hell're you doin' here? Rona Handy said you'd gone after the train.'

'Long story.' Winters suddenly swung the Colt and knocked Endicott to the ground.

Dazed, the colonel sat up groggily, blood streaking his pinched face, but raging fury helping him rapidly recover. 'You dare to strike me?'

'I'm thinking about shooting you.'

'Easy, Brad!' warned the sheriff.

'He won't do anything, Slade, he knows he's already in more trouble than he can shake a stick at.'

'What a fool you are, Winters!'

'Aw, I dunno, Colonel, I reckon you'll have a deal of trouble explaining your breach of the rules with this dawn sneak attack. I'll bet your friends at West Point have a lot more scruples and honour than you. And you broke The Code — gave your word, then went back on it. A couple of hundred people must've heard Big Joe give your orders to destroy the Rebel camp. How d'you rate your chances now, Colonel?'

'How would you know anything about The Point?'

'I know that you're a lousy representative of it, Endicott, but you'd be a lousy representative of a Mexican chaingang.'

The colonel's nostrils were pinched

white. He was seething, but had enough sense not to push Winters much harder: the man was close to killing him. *He could sense it!*

'I consider it my mandate to set things to rights with the so-called Battle of Hashknife Ridge. Lord above! Even the name is revolting.'

'You're a damn fool if you think you'd get any recognition for what you've done this morning. This is only a stage-play, nothing more. Yankees 'winning' here is as meaningless as replaying the Little Big Horn with Custer triumphant.'

Endicott's face was murderous. 'You should've died this morning!'

Winters suddenly realized that that had been part of the man's plan. Then Slade Samson jammed his gun into Endicott's side. 'Time you shut your mouth, Colonel.'

'Sheriff's right.' Brad agreed. 'Every time you speak you dig your own grave deeper. You ought to be worrying about your court martial. Your career's finished, Endicott.'

The colonel, for a moment, looked as if he would spring at Winters' throat. Brad was sure he wanted to but suddenly, something snapped in Endicott and he seemed to collapse inwardly.

'What's wrong, Colonel? Just remembered you're a serving army officer? Which means a full-blown court martial, not just a closed hearing with your brother officers. All those old moustache-twirling generals, knowing nothing but Rules-by-the-Book, and the Honour of the Point and all that moral stuff you seem to think nothing of — they're gonna nail your hide to the wall, Endicott. They'll never speak your name again without wanting to spit.'

The colonel made a growling sound deep in his throat and there was even a little froth at one corner of his mouth as he lunged at Brad Winters. The Sheriff casually tripped him and he fell flat on his face. The lawman planted a boot between the man's shoulders — and not gently.

'Just stay put, Yankee. You about

finished, Brad? We'll have to get after that money.'

'We will. That's one more thing our colonel has to answer for, too.'

Matt Farrell blinked. 'I thought Tibbetts stole the money?'

'He did — by arrangement with Endicott. Just one more jab at the South, Matt. Steal every cent raised by staging this Battle Day.'

'How would Endicott know Tibbetts?'

'From army patrols into the Cherokee Strip, outlaw country. He could've easily made a deal — but forget the details for now, we still have to recover the money.'

'Thought that's what you were doin',' Slade said. 'The Handy gal told us Tibbetts got away on the train and you'd gone after him.'

'It started out that way. Like me, Ethan Handy and even the train crew thought Tibbetts and his gang were riding in the caboose with the loot.'

Samson frowned. 'But we heard the train pull out!'

'You were meant to: it's a decoy. Everyone would believe the thieves would make their getaway on the train and a posse would go after it.'

'Well, what the hell did happen?' The sheriff's impatience was making him shout.

'Wiley was the only one of the robbers to go on board the train. He told the crew Tibbetts and the others were in the caboose and ordered the driver to keep the train going flat out until he told him to stop. Then he dropped off the train out of their sight. But I saw him and we had a shoot-out. Before he died, Wiley told me Tibbetts and the others dressed in Yankee uniforms taken from Bede Halstrom's store, and came out here.'

'To Hashknife?' Farrell asked incredulously. 'Why?'

'So they could lose themselves amongst the re-enactors, mingle and ride out after Battle Day, just like the other Yankees going home. It's one reason Endicott staged the dawn raid, gave them a chance to lose themselves more easily in the Union ranks while the posse was busting its butt chasing after the Denver train, miles away.'

A lot of eyes were on Endicott now but he refused to look at anyone, closed his eyes and tightened his lips: hell, there was nothing he could say.

Suddenly, Kit Turner, in the crowd that had gathered, called, 'Brad! There! It's Griffin!'

The crowd suddenly scattered like ants from a crumbling anthill as gunshots roared. Turner spun violently, fell to his knees, arm bleeding.

Brad saw Griffin then, shoving and bulling and gunwhipping his way through blood-streaked, battered men. There was another disturbance to the left. Tibbetts and Chip Durant were running downhill, no doubt making for horses already waiting in the timber.

Brad drew his six-gun and yelled for the crowd to make way, sprinting forward for the Arab horse. Samson, neckerchief tied round his arm now, followed him. Durant turned on the run, snapped two fast shots. A man wearing a Confederate uniform stumbled and fell. Samson triggered in return.

'Hold it, Slade!' yelled Winters. 'There're innocent men down there.'

'Then they better learn how to duck!' the sheriff snapped, limping along as fast as he could.

Matt Farrell, head still bleeding, came crashing through on his mount, tossed Brad a Winchester and wheeled towards Reed Galvin who was trying to escape unnoticed. But Matt had spotted him and shot him in the upper thigh. The man went down, grimacing, bringing up his Sheriff's Special. Brad whipped his rifle to his shoulder and a bullet slammed into Reed's chest, driving him down. Kit Turner, despite his arm wound was trying to find a safe angle he could shoot at the fleeing thieves without endangering innocent lives.

Chip Durant grabbed a woman spectator who had fallen in her hurry to run away. He held her close to him as he slid down into the draw. A man in Confederate uniform, probably her husband, ran forward to help. Durant shot him coldly. The woman fainted. Her sudden dead weight dragged Durant off-balance. He fell to one knee and swung up his gun desperately.

Winters rode him down mercilessly, the impact throwing the killer against a tree. Dazed, he still tried to use his six-gun and Matt Farrell shot him and rode on by.

Tibbetts and Griffin were in amongst the trees now, running for a small dry wash. Brad figured their getaway mounts were in there. Handy's Arab stallion was fighting the bit now, foam flying from its mouth, unused to such rough treatment. Brad refrained from using the spurs, slid out of the saddle, rifle in hand. He skidded on gravel, righted himself, and ran after the fugitives. Griffin saw him coming, turned and triggered, fanning the hammer, Colt bucking. Brad dived for cover and when he looked up again, Griffin had disappeared into the dry wash, hard on the heels of Tibbetts.

Matt Farrell felt suddenly dizzy and fell sideways out of the saddle, crashing into nearby brush, the horse running on. As Matt lay there, dazed and winded, Slade Samson slipped and slid down the slope, launched himself at the reins of Matt's mount. He surprised himself by catching them and tried to calm the animal so he could climb into the saddle. Matt waved him on and Brad ran back to the Arab.

Other men were sliding down the slopes, too, eager to help, but most hit the dirt when real bullets began to fly. Women on the hillside shouted at their menfolk to stay out of it, to leave the fighting to those who knew what they were doing.

Both blue and grey soldiers were gathered on a slope and when some of the Union men grabbed the chance to get to a safer position, a Confederate voice said, loudly, 'Someone got their colours mixed-up, fellers — it ain't 'blue-bellies', it should be 'yaller bellies'!'

In seconds the hillside was covered with jostling, struggling punching men and the fighting started up again, right across Hashknife Ridge.

Spud Bromley and a group of eager Confederates loaded the second cannon with a charge of black-powder, then half-filled the barrel with river sand. They fought it around to the nearest slope where a lot of men were brawling, and lit the fuse. The gun thundered, spewing a massive cloud of thick smoke and a jet of stinging sand. Men yelled and danced in agony, broke off the fighting, clawing at eyes and stinging flesh. They looked at each others' fresh wounds and one man spat a tooth, saying, 'Well, it's still not as painful as losin' it to that goddamn dentist in town!'

Silence. Then someone began to chuckle and it spread, others took it up and the feeble joke was later credited as bringing calm to the battlefield.

'Why don't you blamed fools call it a draw and be done with it?' called one of the wives and others took up the cry and 'Draw' became a chant that rolled down the slopes until someone finally said, 'OK! OK! It's a goddamn draw! Will that keep you quiet?'

It did and soon tobacco was being passed back and forth between Union and Confederate and the womenfolk heaved sighs of relief and congratulated each other on bringing an end to the Battle of Hashknife Ridge, 1879.

But Winters and Samson knew nothing about this as they rammed their mounts into the dry wash where the thieves had gone.

And both men almost died on the spot.

Tibbetts and Griffin were already mounted, saddle-bags bulging, each leading a second horse — likely the ones that had belonged to Durant and Galvin — they wouldn't be needing them. Yelling wildly, the outlaws charged. There was a tangle of whinnying, thrashing, biting mounts, men standing in the stirrups as they tried to control the animals. Guns fired wildly as the outlaws smashed their way through.

Griffin slashed at Brad with his smoking Colt but the ramrod ducked in time. Then Griffin bulled his way past and Winters' horse started to go down. He slid around the belly and, as it rose, stepped expertly back into the saddle: an old cowman's trick, but not many could pull it off successfully.

The horse surged up under him and he turned across the draw after the fugitives. Dust was thick and powder-smoke still hung in the air. He resisted the urge to shoot in case he hit Samson. Then he saw the two robbers splashing across the river ford. He spurred after them. They were halfway across now, but had just missed the ford so that their horses were swimming in deep water. Tibbetts got his mount up onto the ford, but Griffin had a fight on his hands.

Brad fired just as his own mount stepped off the bank into the river: he missed. Once on the ford he triggered again and Griffin reeled. Tibbetts stayed well clear so that he was out of danger from any stray lead: plainly, it was every man for himself as far as Mort Tibbetts was concerned.

Brad's next shot knocked Griffin forward and the man clawed desperately at the saddlehorn, half his body slipping into the river. He let go the reins, struggled to bring up his dripping Colt. Winters charged alongside and shot Griffin through the middle of the face. He sheathed the rifle, looked across the river: Tibbetts had reached the far bank. He rode into the timber, still leading the second horse. Brad reloaded before riding into the trees, mighty wary, thumb on the rifle's hammer spur. He knew this area well, had started many a hiding maverick out of this brush during round-up. He hauled rein, trying to hear Tibbetts' progress. But his horse was blowing too hard and he touched the spurs lightly to the quivering flanks, walking the mount very cautiously. *Something moved, a glimpse through brush . . . .*

He wrenched the reins, jammed the spurs in hard, and the Arab leapt its own length in one whinnying lunge. He swung it into a swerving, zigzag run, reins gripped in his left hand, lying low in the saddle. But there was no gunfire and after a minute, he slowed, dismounted. Rubbing the horse's foam-caked neck absently, he looked about him, tied the reins to a low branch and went in on foot, crouching.

Movement to the left made him swing that way, bringing up the rifle. Through the vegetation he saw a horse in the clearing, wet from the river. The flaps of the canvas bank bags tied to the saddle were loose — and there was money poking out of the nearest one. A few more bills were scattered on the ground, dropped by Tibbetts in his hurry. He would travel faster, all right, no longer having to lead the second horse — and wouldn't even spare a thought for Griffin.

Brad waited, finally moved slowly towards the horse as it cropped some grass. It looked at him curiously, plainly content to be resting. He spoke softly to it, watching the surrounding brush constantly as he advanced. Then he saw there was only a single ten-dollar bill poking out of the nearest canvas bag — *pinned in place* so it wouldn't blow away, would stay in plain view . . . *Trap!*

The word no sooner crashed into his brain than a rifle blasted a short volley and the decoy horse reared and whinnied briefly as it fell. The ramrod dived hurriedly to the ground as more lead sought him. The horse was down and kicking its last. He saw the hovering cloud of gunsmoke in the trees suddenly shake as Tibbetts triggered again. The bullet thudded into the carcass.

Winters rose swiftly, rifle raking the brush under that pall of smoke with a hammering volley, lever blurring, ejected shell cases glittering in the morning sunlight. Bark, twigs and leaves flew in a chaotic swirl. Tibbetts crashed out of the brush, staggering, blood trickling from a corner of his mouth, more splashed on his neck and chest. His eyes were still wild and murderous as he fought to lift the Colt sagging in his weakening grasp. More blood flooded over his chin. He tried to take one more step, faltered and abruptly collapsed, twisting onto his back.

Winters approached cautiously, but there was no need: Tibbetts was dead.

The sheriff rode in, glanced briefly and without expression at the dead outlaw. 'Kit's watchin' Briscoe and Endicott. You — er — like to spend a little private time with that damn Yankee colonel, be glad to look the other way, Brad.'

Winters shook his head wearily. 'Thanks, but no, Slade. Whatever West Point does to him will settle any old scores. Endicott's career is over.'

'Yeah — helluva shame for a man like him to have to live with — doubt if he can.'

The sheriff was more prophetic than he knew. Two months later, during the first snow of winter, ex-Colonel Kelvin Endicott Junior, hanged himself in the holding cell, while awaiting the Military Court's verdict . . .

★   ★   ★

Later, in the spring, at Brad Winters' suggestion, Matt Farrell erected a flagpole on the knife edge of Hashknife Ridge. A brass plaque, set in cement at the base, contained the names of men killed in the 1864 battle — both Union and Confederate. Heroes all.

'We'll build a fence around it,' Matt said enthusiastically. 'Hold a formal dedication ceremony, at sunset, and invite the Territorial Governor . . . '

'Sorry I'll miss it, Matt,' Winters said, tight-lipped and not sounding in the least sorry, already backing away. 'I've got a trail herd to load on the Denver train. I'm riding up with it, so I better get started.'

'You can deliver the governor's invitation then — I suppose I should invite the Territorial Committee, too. And if Captain Johnson can arrange a march past — Brad! *Brad!* Wait a minute, damnit!'

'I'll miss the train, Matt. *Adios*, I'll see you when I see you!'

And that won't be too damn soon, he added silently, as he vaulted into the saddle and spurred his horse down the slope, away from Hashknife Ridge. *And Farrell's next show.*

THE END

Other titles in the
Linford Western Library:

REMEMBER KETCHELL

Nick Benjamin

The brutal beating from big cattle boss Ethan Amador left cowhand Floyd Ketchell near death: punishment for daring to fall in love with his beautiful daughter, Tara. Now, returning five years later, and a top gunfighter, he wants his revenge. But he finds many changes in the town of Liberty, Texas. Tara, a ranch boss herself, has a handsome hardcase as her right-hand man. Can Ketchell rekindle the fierce passion they had once shared and still kill her father?

MASSACRE AT BLUFF POINT

I. J. Parnham

Ethan Craig has only just started working for Sam Pringle's outfit when Ansel Stark's bandits bushwhack the men at Bluff Point. Ethan's new colleagues are gunned down in cold blood and he vows revenge. But Ethan's manhunt never gets underway — Sheriff Henry Fisher arrests him and he's accused of being a member of the very gang he'd sworn to track down! With nobody believing his innocence and a ruthless bandit to catch, can Ethan ever hope to succeed?